NORTHWEST R...

A Girl Called ECHO

VOL. 3

By Katherena Vermette
Illustrated by Scott B. Henderson
Coloured by Donovan Yaciuk

HIGHWATER
PRESS

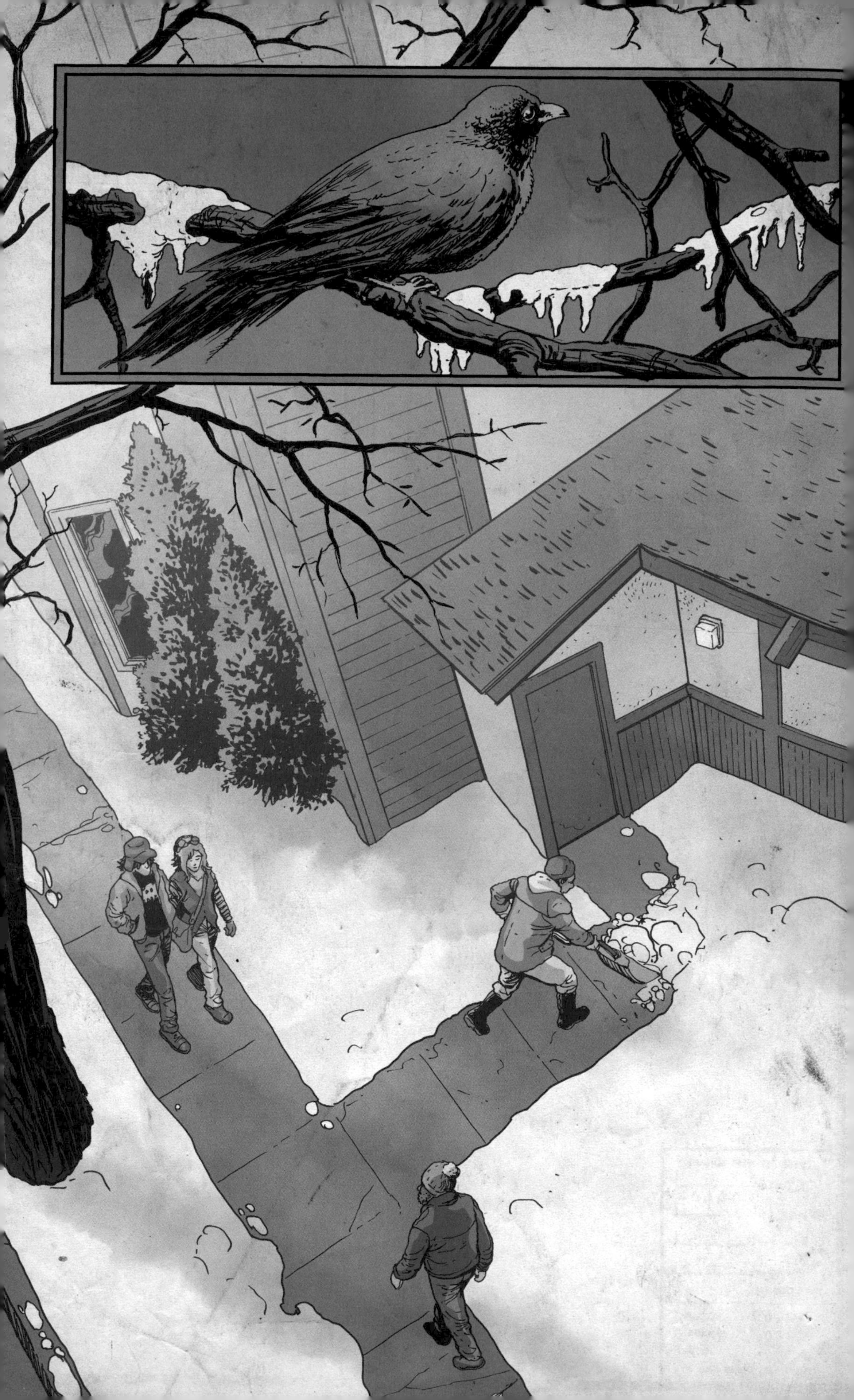

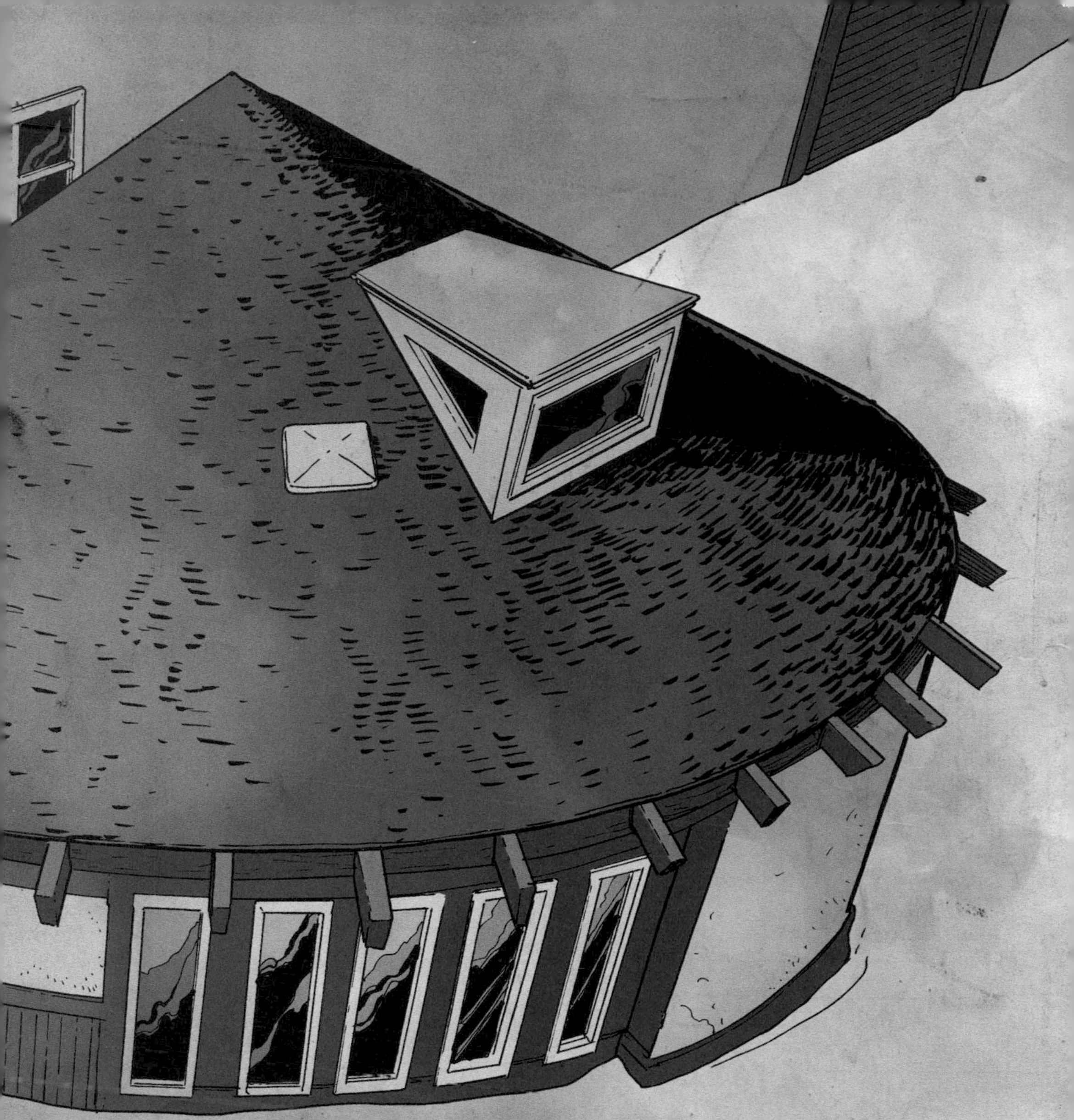

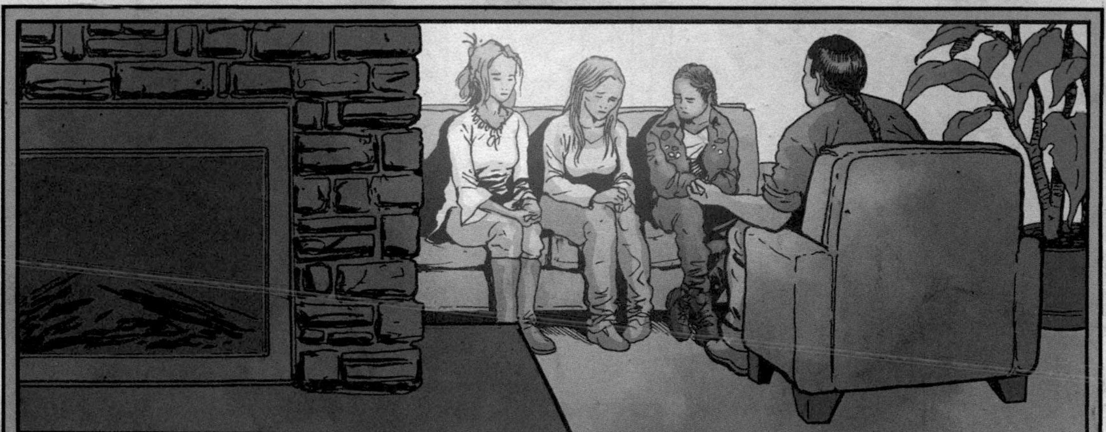

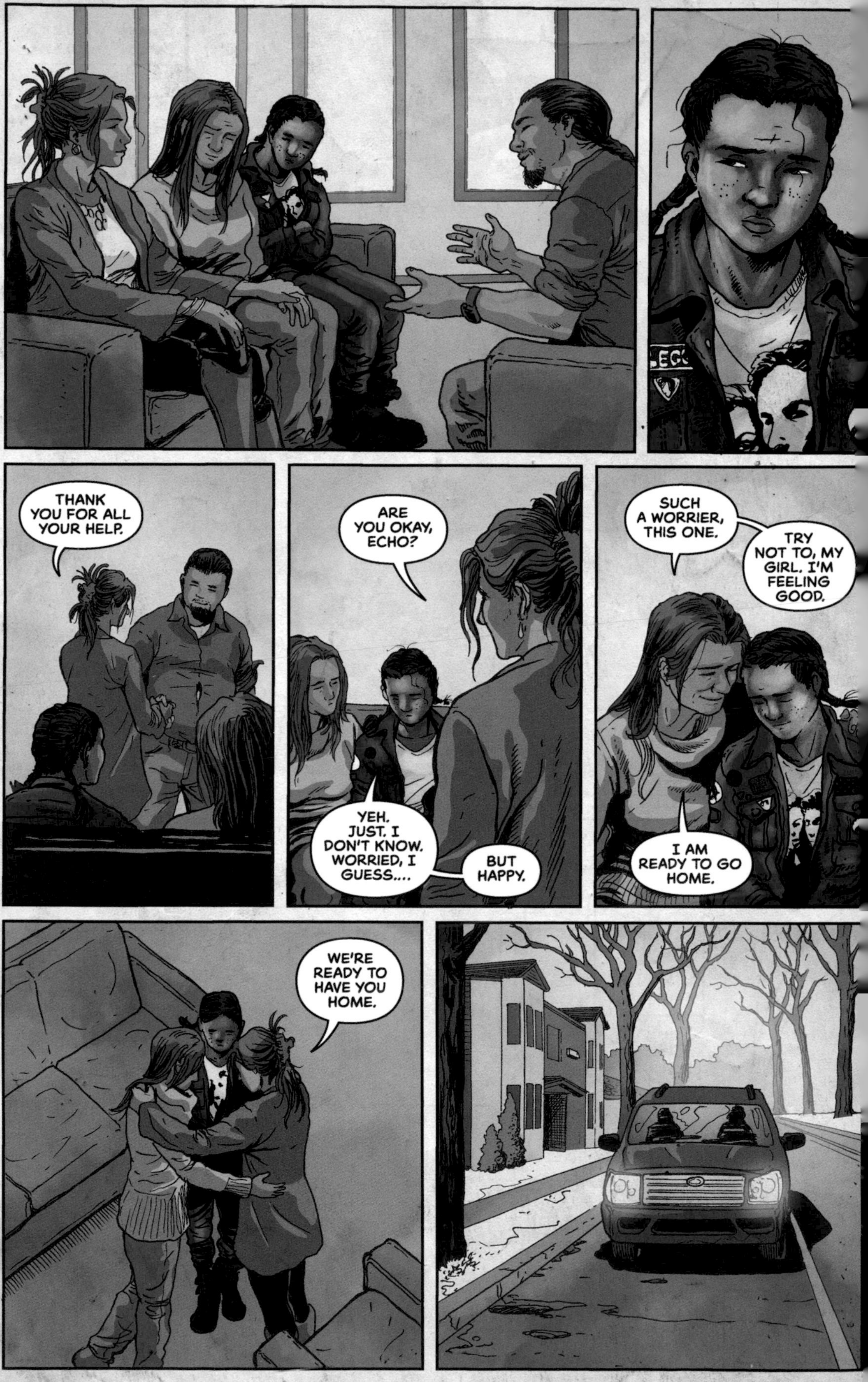
THANK YOU FOR ALL YOUR HELP.
ARE YOU OKAY, ECHO?
YEH. JUST. I DON'T KNOW. WORRIED, I GUESS....
BUT HAPPY.
SUCH A WORRIER, THIS ONE.
TRY NOT TO, MY GIRL. I'M FEELING GOOD.
I AM READY TO GO HOME.
WE'RE READY TO HAVE YOU HOME.

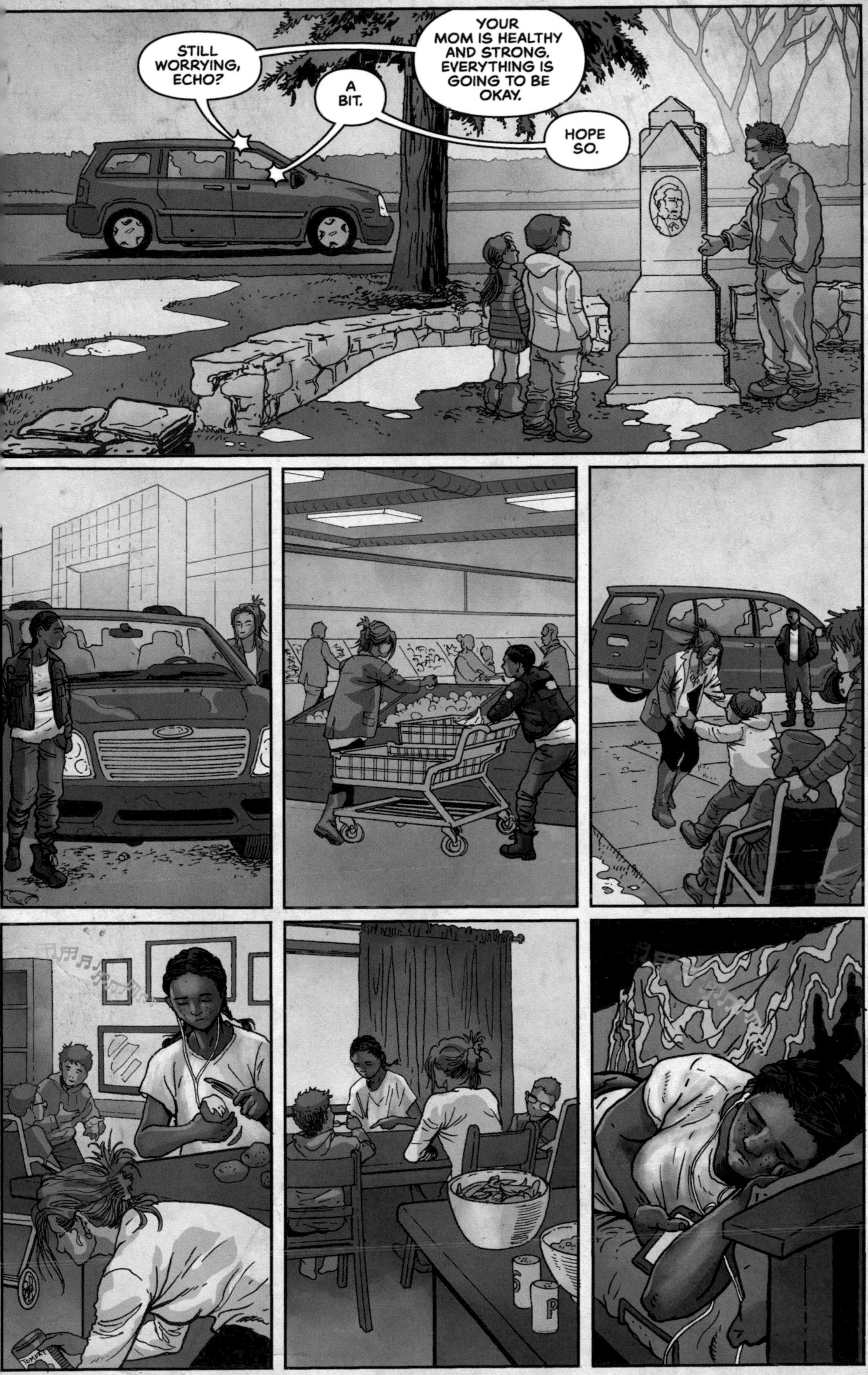
STILL WORRYING, ECHO?
A BIT.
YOUR MOM IS HEALTHY AND STRONG. EVERYTHING IS GOING TO BE OKAY.
HOPE SO.

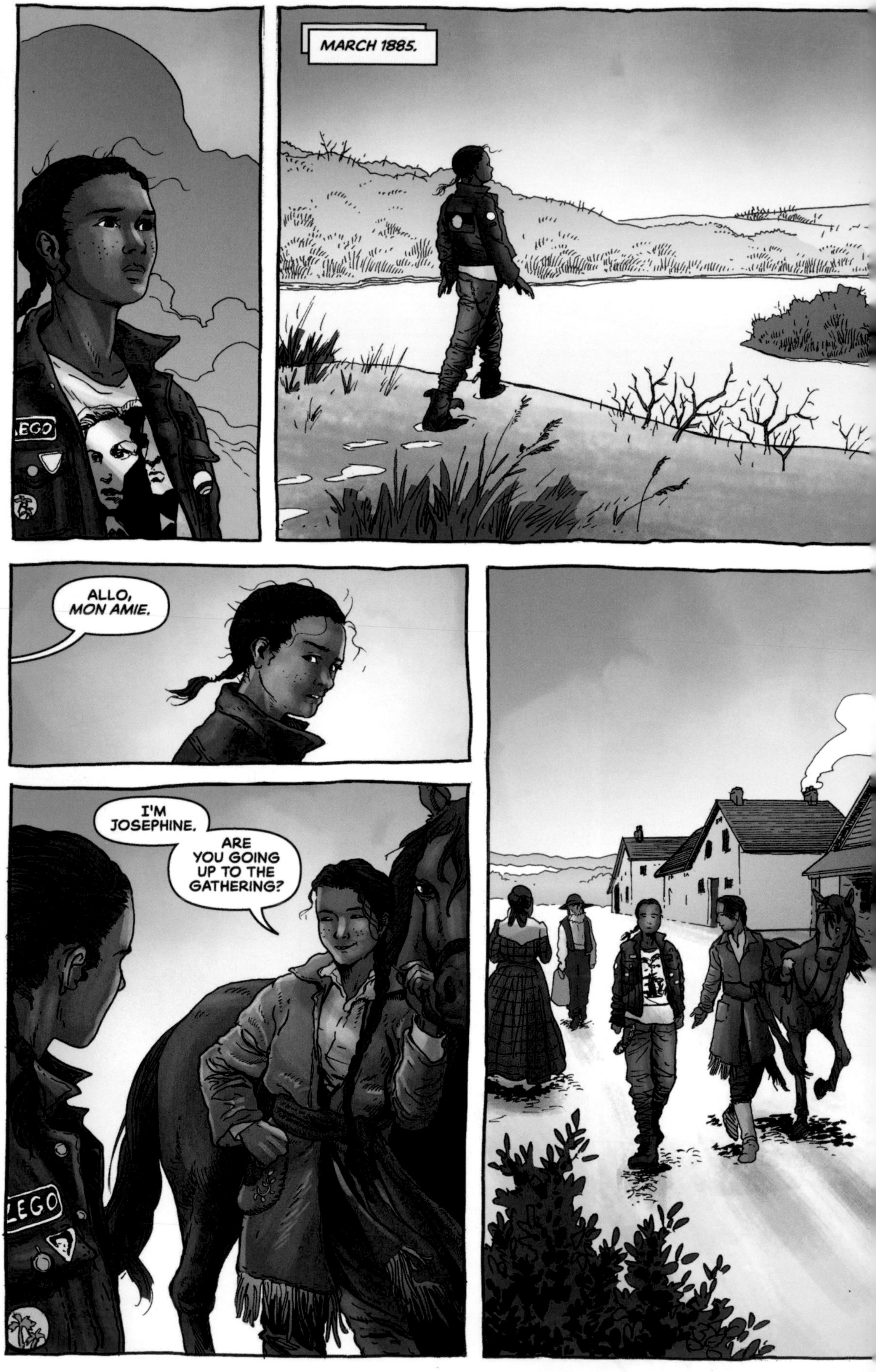
MARCH 1885.
LEGO
ALLO, MON AMIE.
I'M JOSEPHINE.
ARE YOU GOING UP TO THE GATHERING?
LEGO

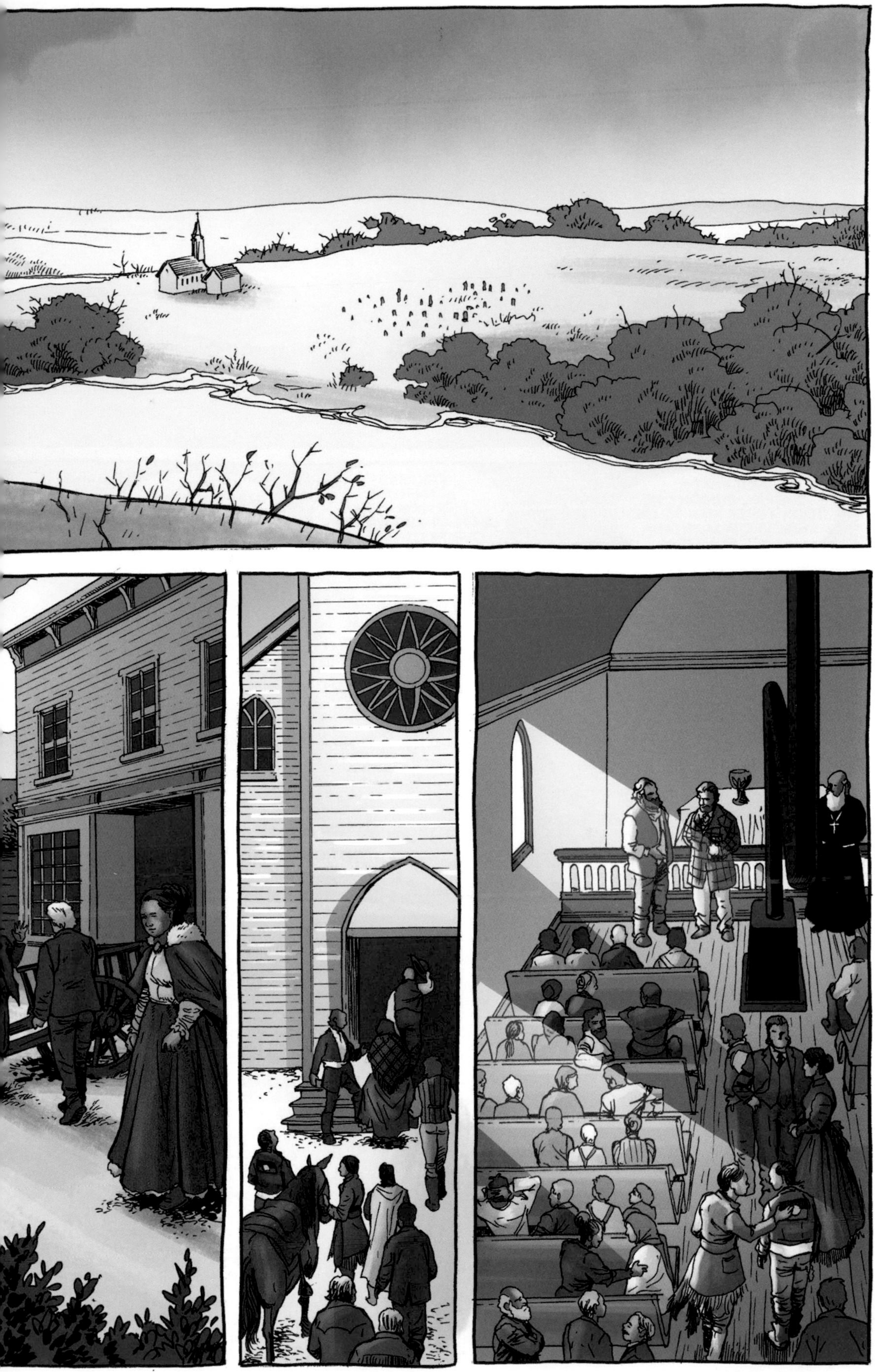

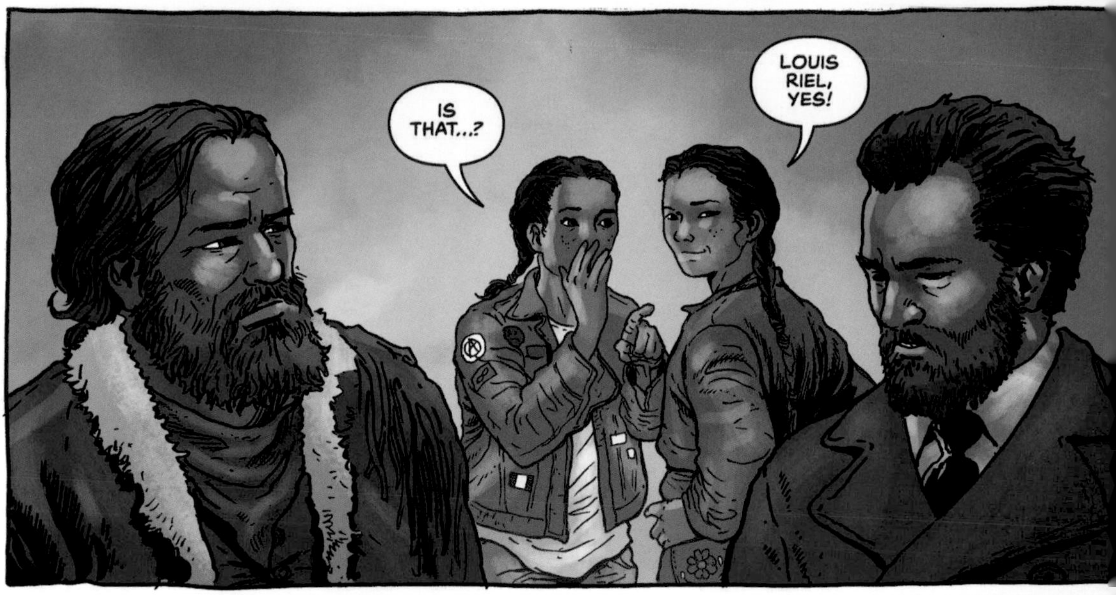
IS THAT...?
LOUIS RIEL, YES!

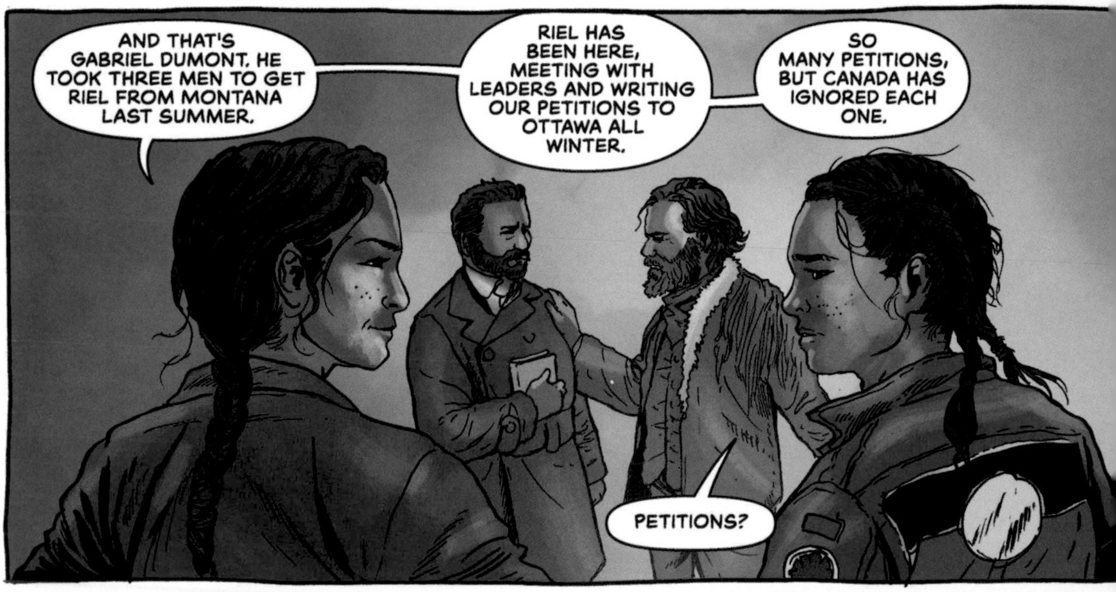
AND THAT'S GABRIEL DUMONT. HE TOOK THREE MEN TO GET RIEL FROM MONTANA LAST SUMMER.
RIEL HAS BEEN HERE, MEETING WITH LEADERS AND WRITING OUR PETITIONS TO OTTAWA ALL WINTER.
SO MANY PETITIONS, BUT CANADA HAS IGNORED EACH ONE.
PETITIONS?

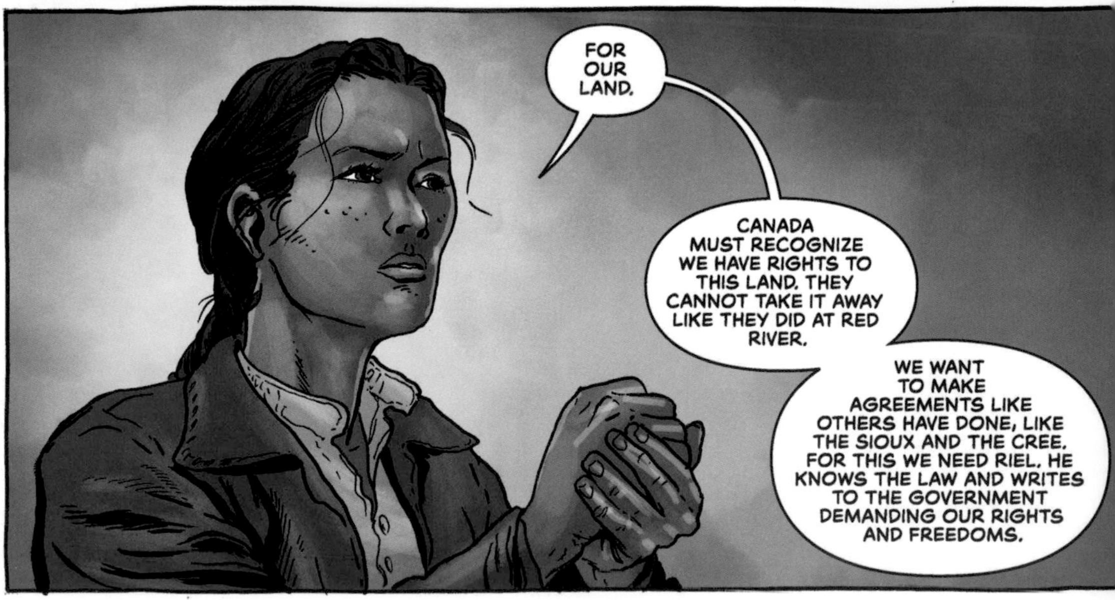
FOR OUR LAND.
CANADA MUST RECOGNIZE WE HAVE RIGHTS TO THIS LAND. THEY CANNOT TAKE IT AWAY LIKE THEY DID AT RED RIVER.
WE WANT TO MAKE AGREEMENTS LIKE OTHERS HAVE DONE, LIKE THE SIOUX AND THE CREE. FOR THIS WE NEED RIEL. HE KNOWS THE LAW AND WRITES TO THE GOVERNMENT DEMANDING OUR RIGHTS AND FREEDOMS.

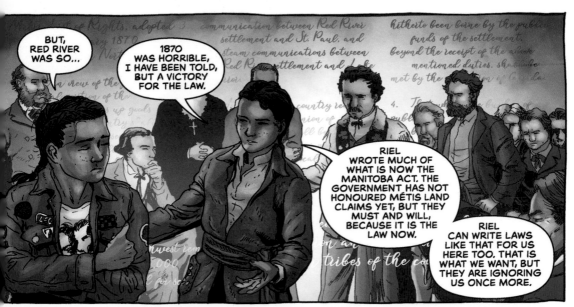

BUT, RED RIVER WAS SO...

1870 WAS HORRIBLE, I HAVE BEEN TOLD, BUT A VICTORY FOR THE LAW.

RIEL WROTE MUCH OF WHAT IS NOW THE MANITOBA ACT. THE GOVERNMENT HAS NOT HONOURED MÉTIS LAND CLAIMS YET, BUT THEY MUST AND WILL, BECAUSE IT IS THE LAW NOW.

RIEL CAN WRITE LAWS LIKE THAT FOR US HERE TOO. THAT IS WHAT WE WANT, BUT THEY ARE IGNORING US ONCE MORE.

YOU'RE SO... DETERMINED.

OF COURSE WE ARE, WE ARE IN THE RIGHT.

AND WE CAN DEFEND OUR RIGHTS, TOO. WE DON'T WANT TO, BUT WE WILL.

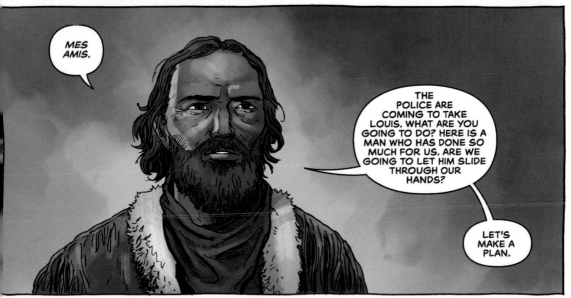

MES AMIS.

THE POLICE ARE COMING TO TAKE LOUIS. WHAT ARE YOU GOING TO DO? HERE IS A MAN WHO HAS DONE SO MUCH FOR US. ARE WE GOING TO LET HIM SLIDE THROUGH OUR HANDS?

LET'S MAKE A PLAN.

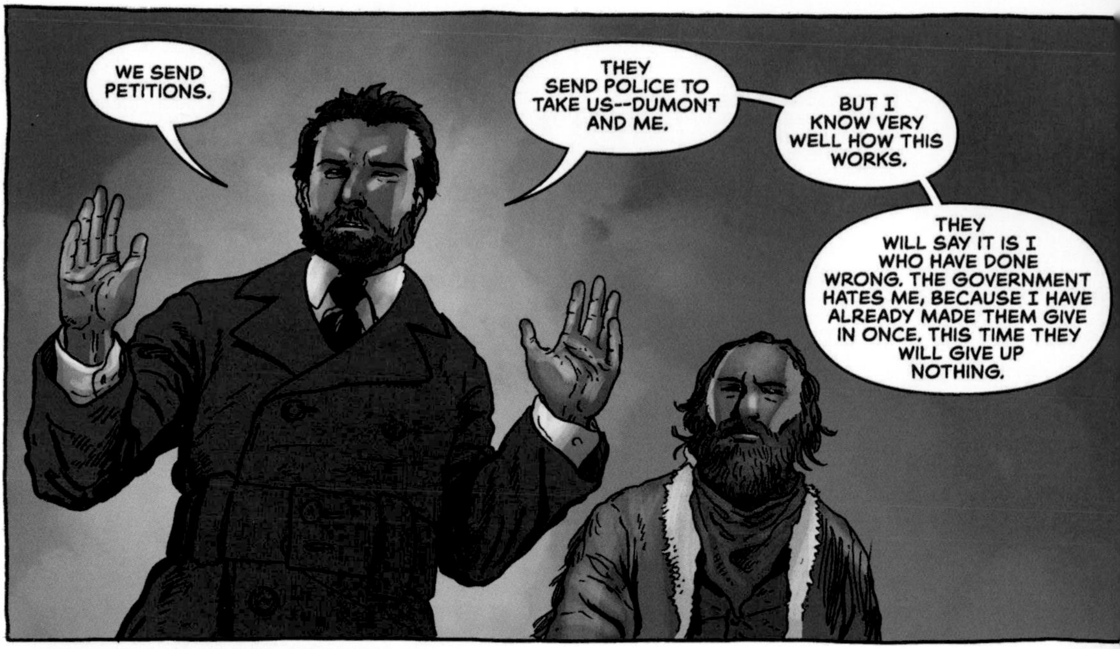
WE SEND PETITIONS.
THEY SEND POLICE TO TAKE US--DUMONT AND ME.
BUT I KNOW VERY WELL HOW THIS WORKS.
THEY WILL SAY IT IS I WHO HAVE DONE WRONG. THE GOVERNMENT HATES ME, BECAUSE I HAVE ALREADY MADE THEM GIVE IN ONCE. THIS TIME THEY WILL GIVE UP NOTHING.

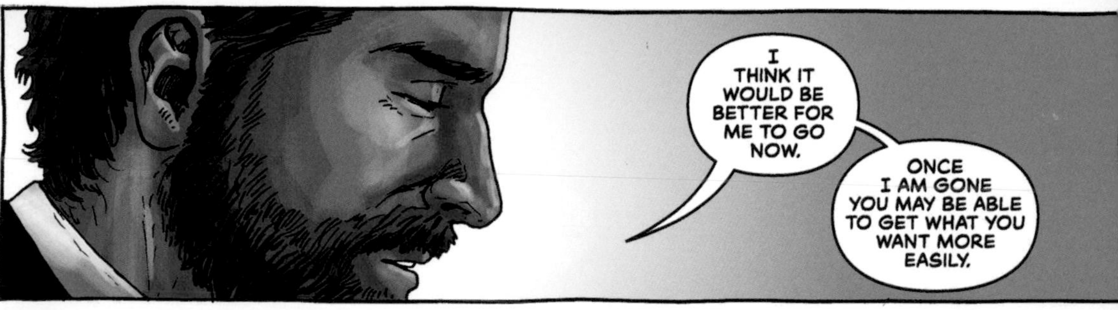
I THINK IT WOULD BE BETTER FOR ME TO GO NOW.
ONCE I AM GONE YOU MAY BE ABLE TO GET WHAT YOU WANT MORE EASILY.

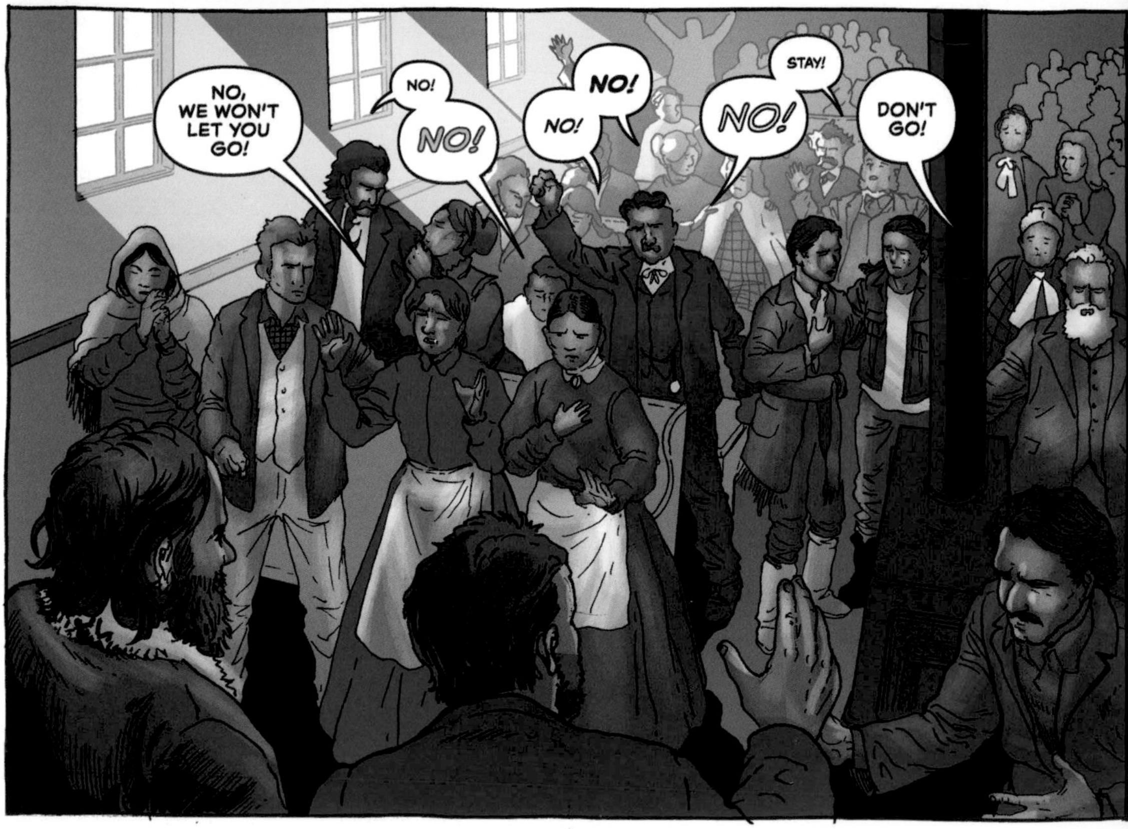
NO, WE WON'T LET YOU GO!
NO!
NO!
NO!
NO!
STAY!
NO!
DON'T GO!

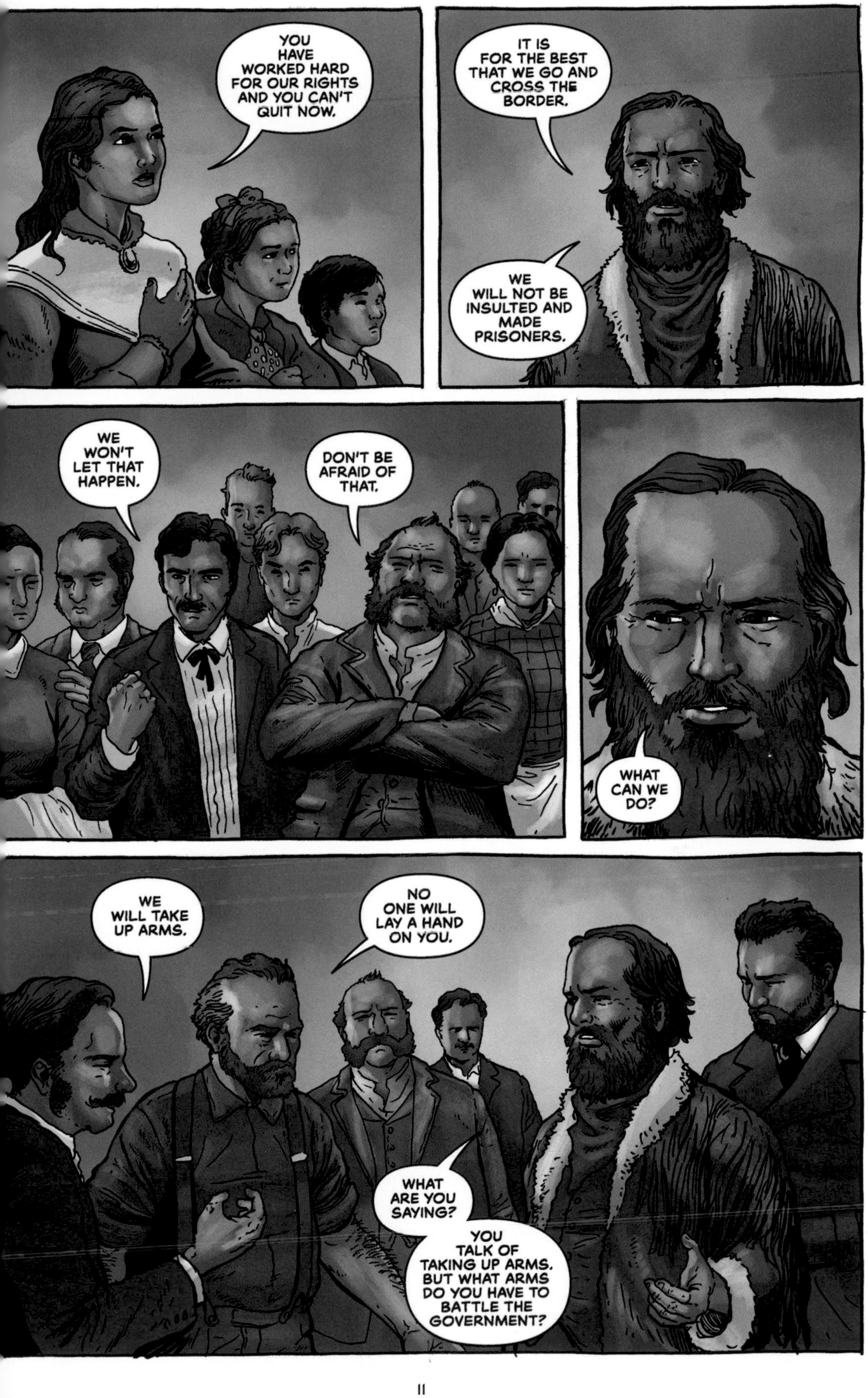
YOU HAVE WORKED HARD FOR OUR RIGHTS AND YOU CAN'T QUIT NOW.
IT IS FOR THE BEST THAT WE GO AND CROSS THE BORDER.
WE WILL NOT BE INSULTED AND MADE PRISONERS.
WE WON'T LET THAT HAPPEN.
DON'T BE AFRAID OF THAT.
WHAT CAN WE DO?
WE WILL TAKE UP ARMS.
NO ONE WILL LAY A HAND ON YOU.
WHAT ARE YOU SAYING?
YOU TALK OF TAKING UP ARMS. BUT WHAT ARMS DO YOU HAVE TO BATTLE THE GOVERNMENT?

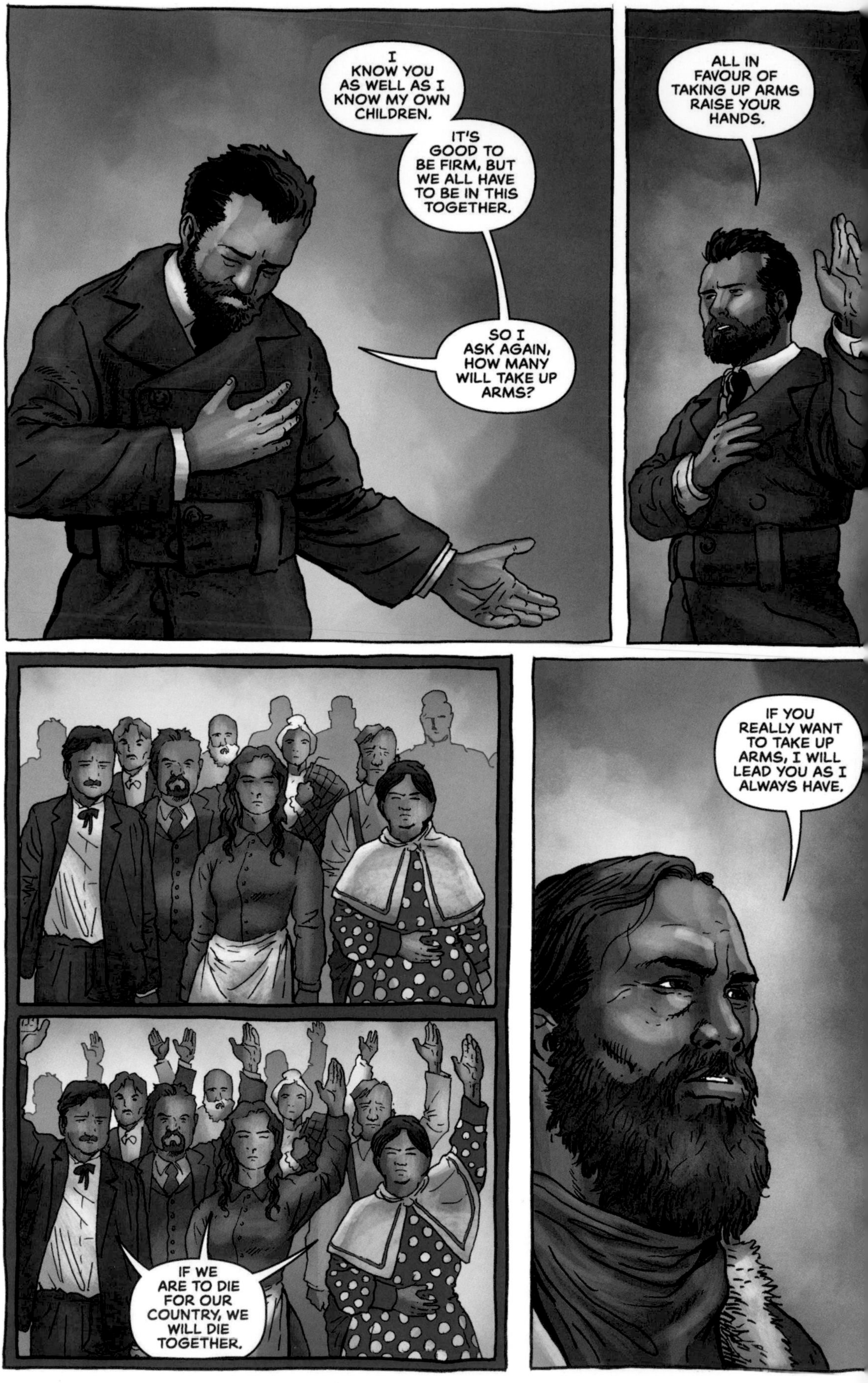
I KNOW YOU AS WELL AS I KNOW MY OWN CHILDREN.
IT'S GOOD TO BE FIRM, BUT WE ALL HAVE TO BE IN THIS TOGETHER.
SO I ASK AGAIN, HOW MANY WILL TAKE UP ARMS?
ALL IN FAVOUR OF TAKING UP ARMS RAISE YOUR HANDS.
IF WE ARE TO DIE FOR OUR COUNTRY, WE WILL DIE TOGETHER.
IF YOU REALLY WANT TO TAKE UP ARMS, I WILL LEAD YOU AS I ALWAYS HAVE.

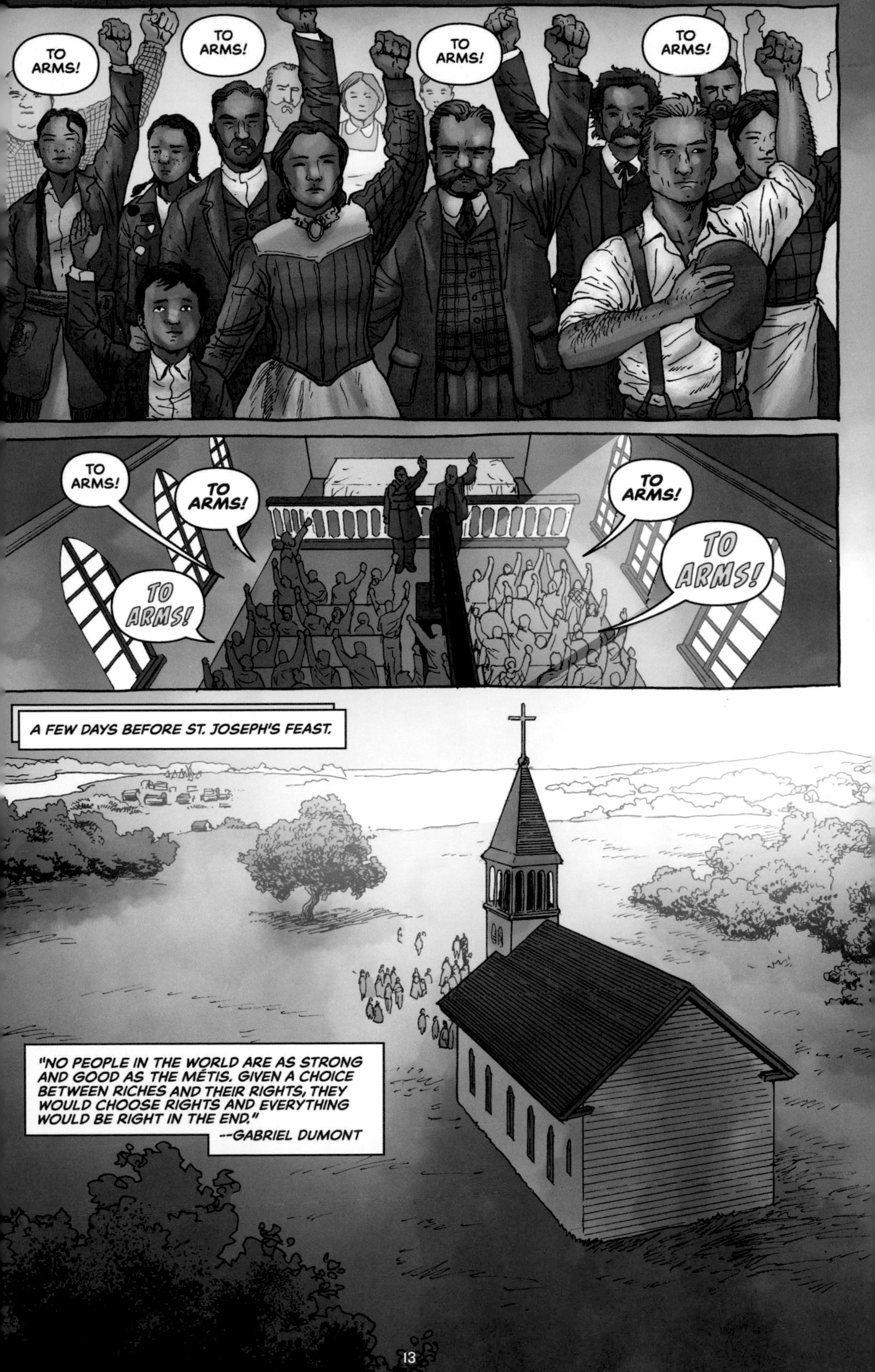
TO ARMS!
TO ARMS!
TO ARMS!
TO ARMS!
TO ARMS!
TO ARMS!
TO ARMS!
TO ARMS!
TO ARMS!
A FEW DAYS BEFORE ST. JOSEPH'S FEAST.
"NO PEOPLE IN THE WORLD ARE AS STRONG AND GOOD AS THE MÉTIS. GIVEN A CHOICE BETWEEN RICHES AND THEIR RIGHTS, THEY WOULD CHOOSE RIGHTS AND EVERYTHING WOULD BE RIGHT IN THE END."
--GABRIEL DUMONT

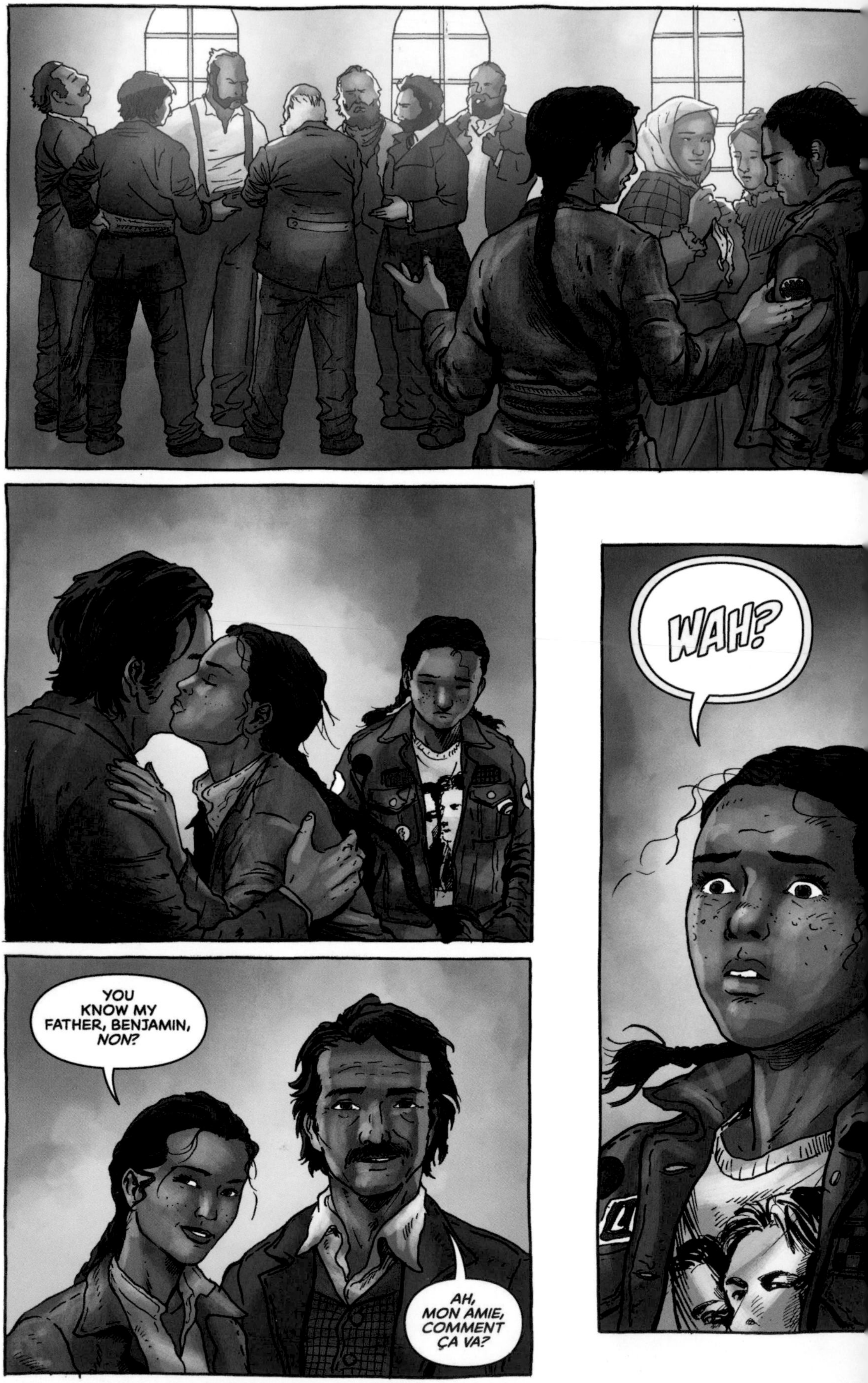
YOU KNOW MY FATHER, BENJAMIN, NON?
AH, MON AMIE, COMMENT ÇA VA?
WAH?

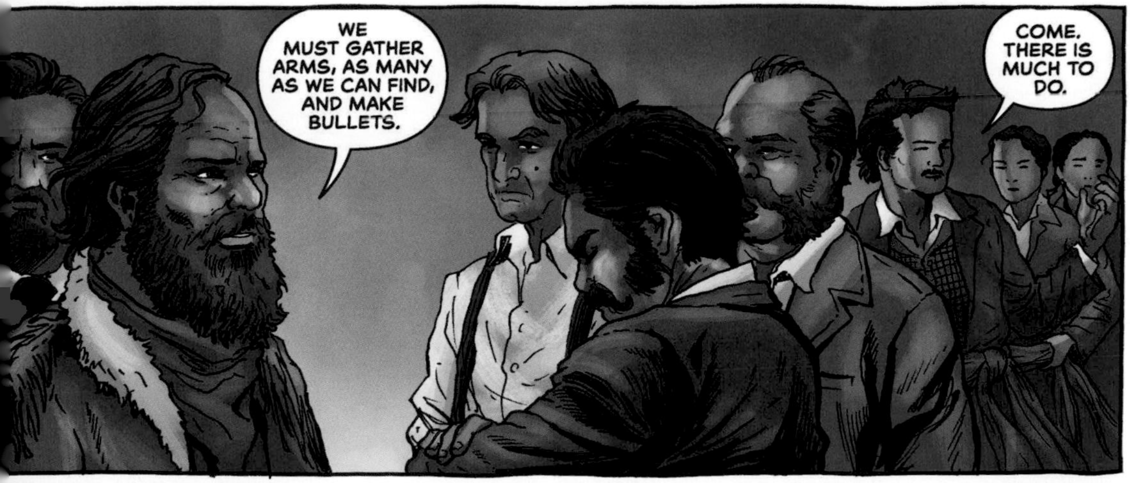
WE MUST GATHER ARMS, AS MANY AS WE CAN FIND, AND MAKE BULLETS.
COME. THERE IS MUCH TO DO.

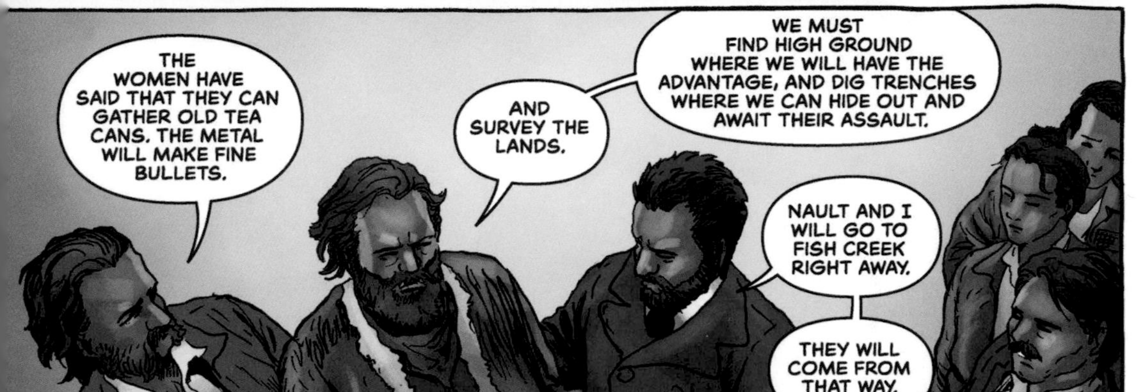
THE WOMEN HAVE SAID THAT THEY CAN GATHER OLD TEA CANS. THE METAL WILL MAKE FINE BULLETS.
AND SURVEY THE LANDS.
WE MUST FIND HIGH GROUND WHERE WE WILL HAVE THE ADVANTAGE, AND DIG TRENCHES WHERE WE CAN HIDE OUT AND AWAIT THEIR ASSAULT.
NAULT AND I WILL GO TO FISH CREEK RIGHT AWAY.
THEY WILL COME FROM THAT WAY.
I WILL GO TO OUR COUSIN WHITE CAP. HE IS OUR CLOSEST NEIGHBOUR.
AND, OUR FRIENDS, WE MUST GATHER THE SETTLERS, THE CREE AND SIOUX BANDS ALL TOGETHER, HERE IN BATOCHE.

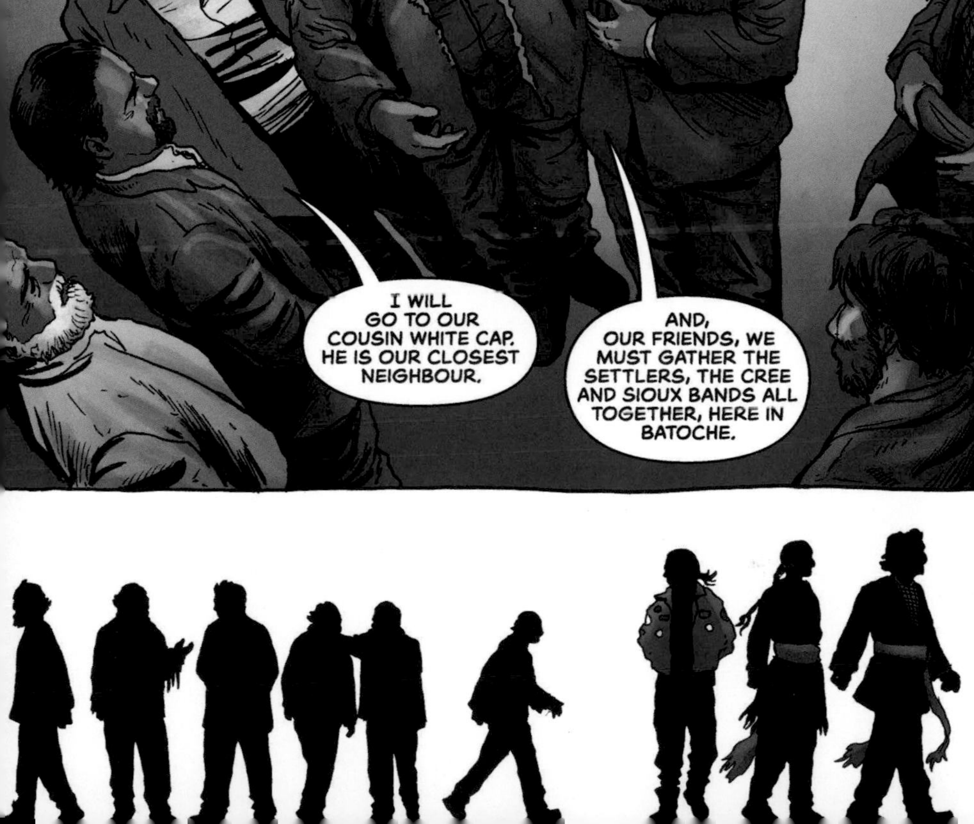

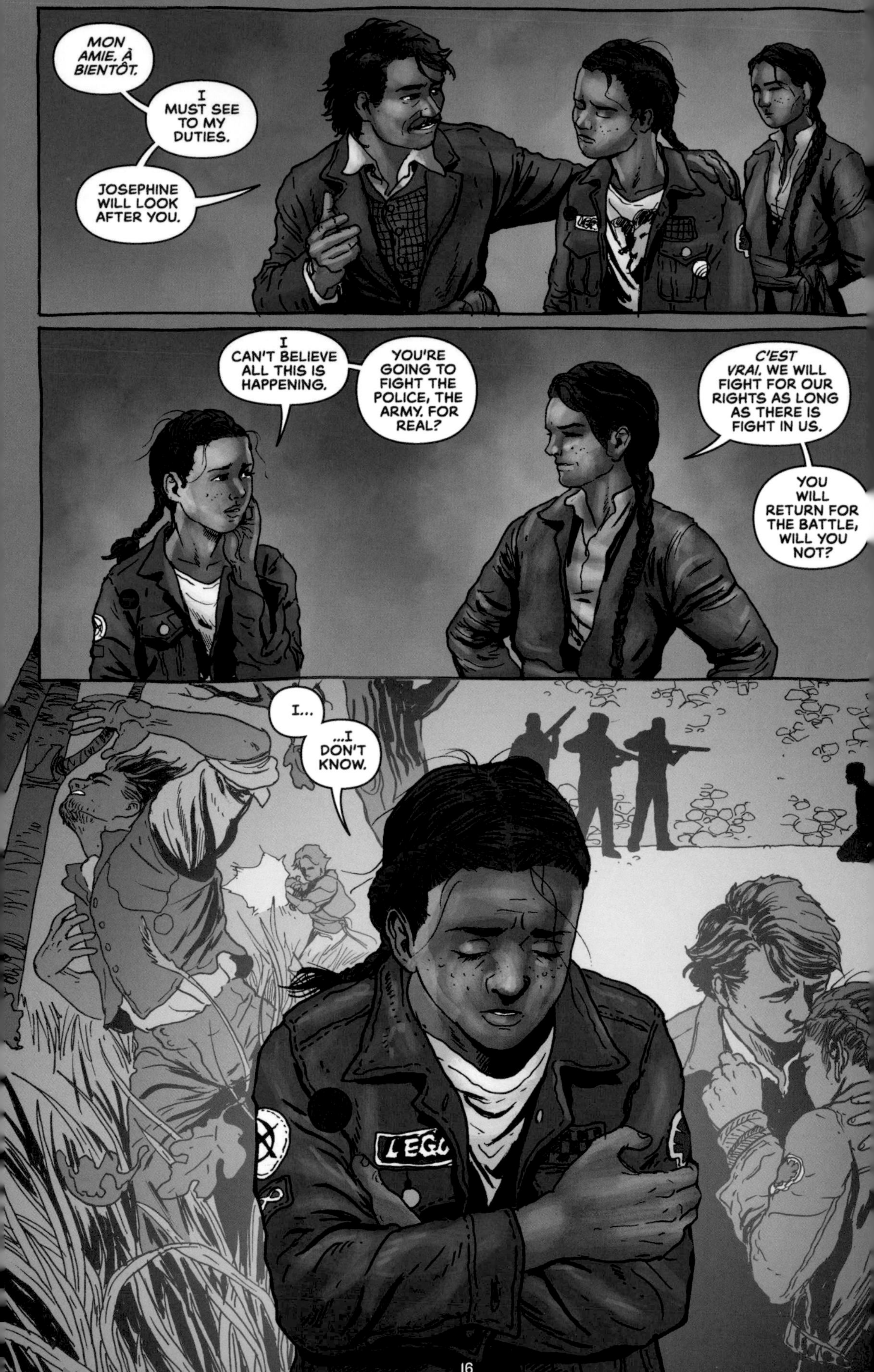
MON AMIE. À BIENTÔT.
I MUST SEE TO MY DUTIES.
JOSEPHINE WILL LOOK AFTER YOU.
I CAN'T BELIEVE ALL THIS IS HAPPENING.
YOU'RE GOING TO FIGHT THE POLICE, THE ARMY. FOR REAL?
C'EST VRAI. WE WILL FIGHT FOR OUR RIGHTS AS LONG AS THERE IS FIGHT IN US.
YOU WILL RETURN FOR THE BATTLE, WILL YOU NOT?
I...
...I DON'T KNOW.
LEGO

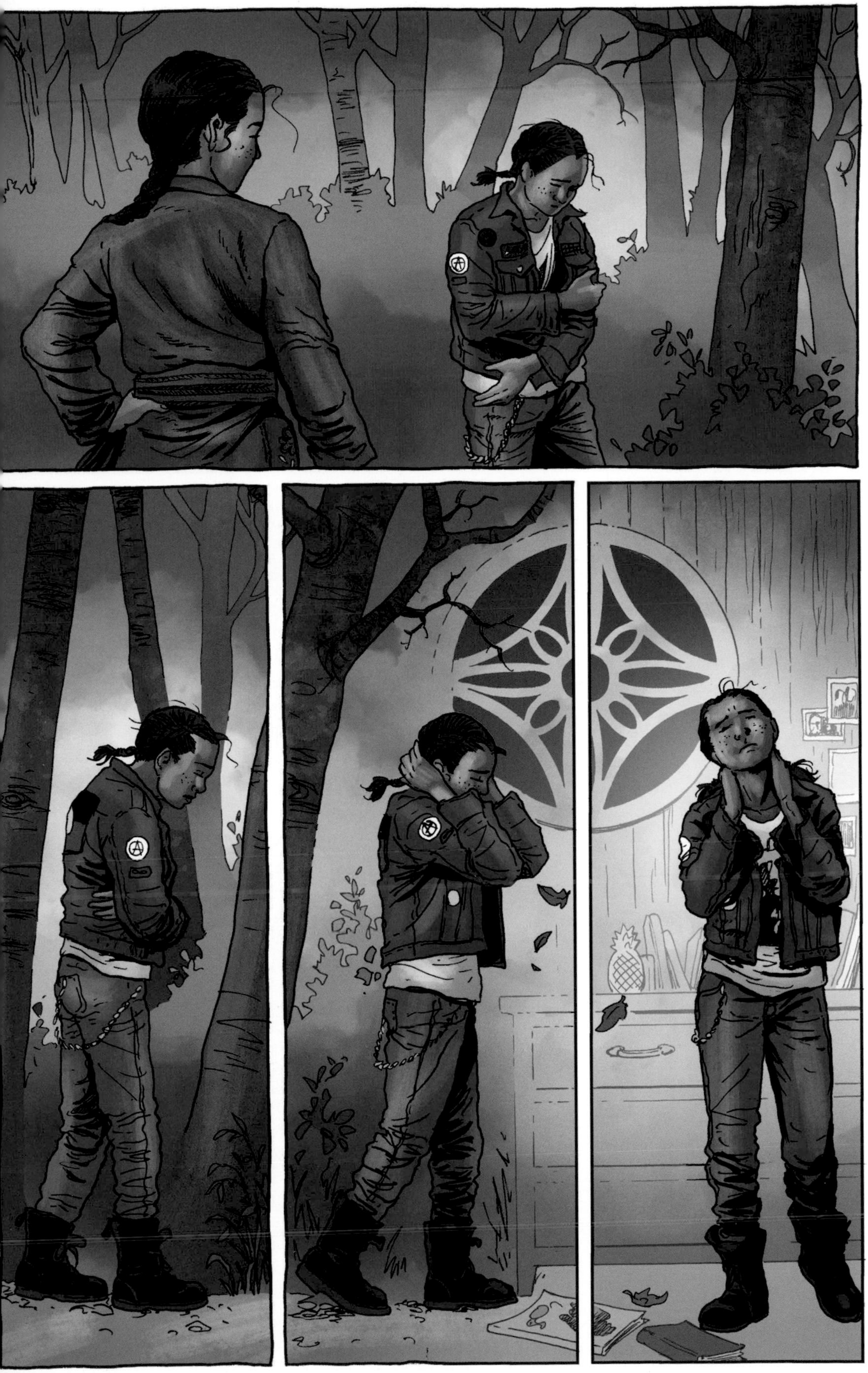

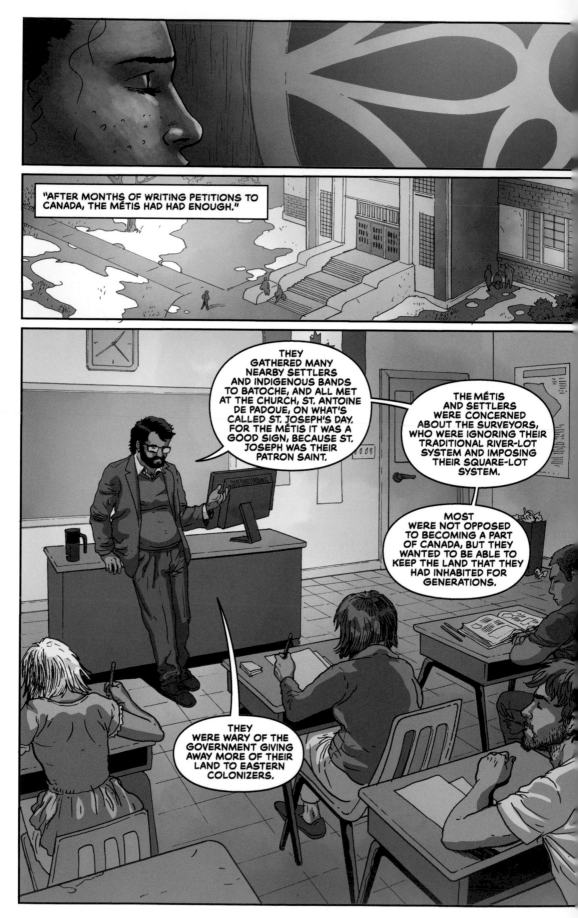

"AFTER MONTHS OF WRITING PETITIONS TO CANADA, THE MÉTIS HAD HAD ENOUGH."

THEY GATHERED MANY NEARBY SETTLERS AND INDIGENOUS BANDS TO BATOCHE, AND ALL MET AT THE CHURCH, ST. ANTOINE DE PADOUE, ON WHAT'S CALLED ST. JOSEPH'S DAY. FOR THE MÉTIS IT WAS A GOOD SIGN, BECAUSE ST. JOSEPH WAS THEIR PATRON SAINT.

THE MÉTIS AND SETTLERS WERE CONCERNED ABOUT THE SURVEYORS, WHO WERE IGNORING THEIR TRADITIONAL RIVER-LOT SYSTEM AND IMPOSING THEIR SQUARE-LOT SYSTEM.

MOST WERE NOT OPPOSED TO BECOMING A PART OF CANADA, BUT THEY WANTED TO BE ABLE TO KEEP THE LAND THAT THEY HAD INHABITED FOR GENERATIONS.

THEY WERE WARY OF THE GOVERNMENT GIVING AWAY MORE OF THEIR LAND TO EASTERN COLONIZERS.

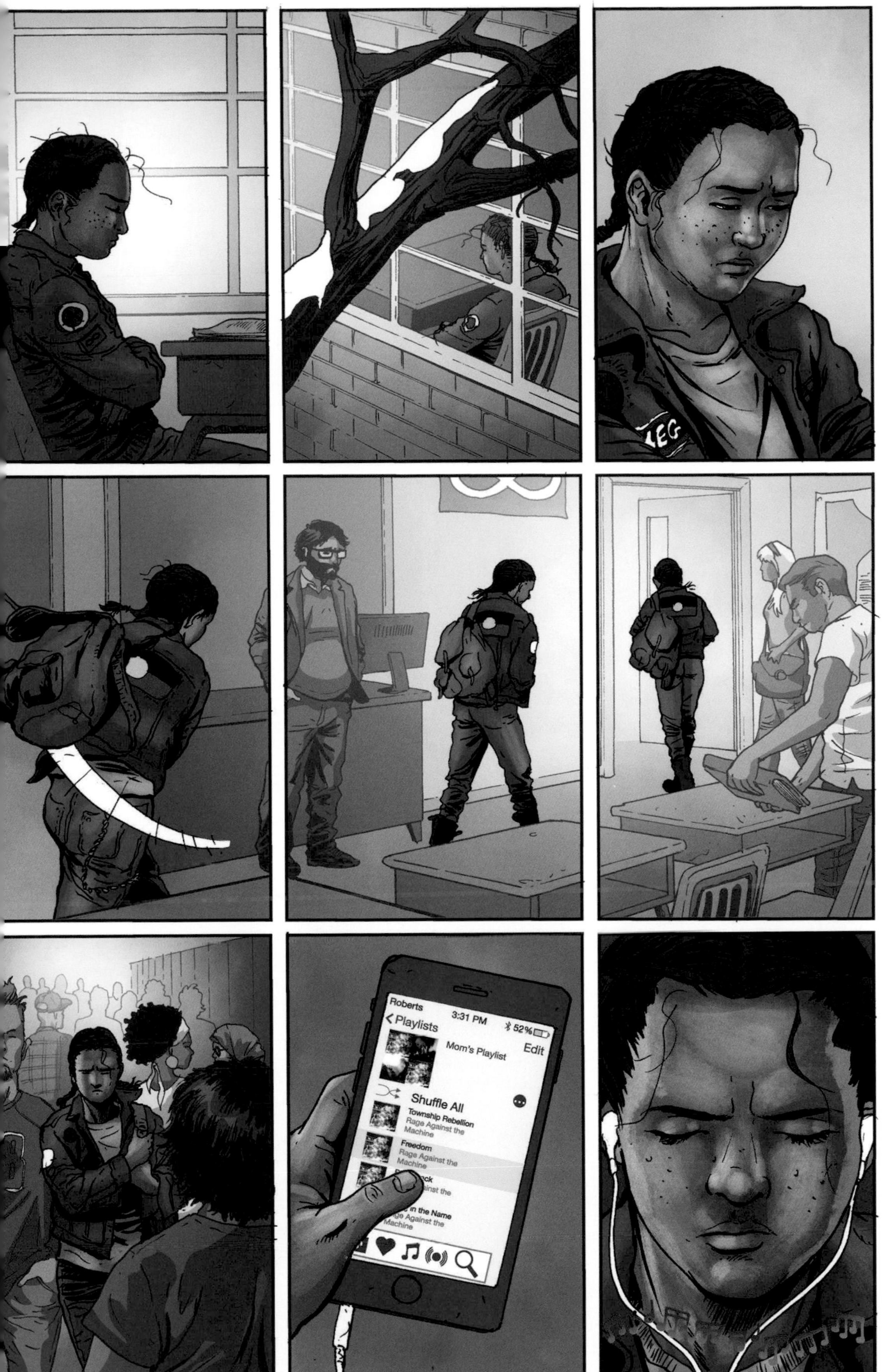
Roberts
3:31 PM
52%
Playlists
Mom's Playlist
Edit
Shuffle All
Township Rebellion
Rage Against the Machine
Freedom
Rage Against the Machine

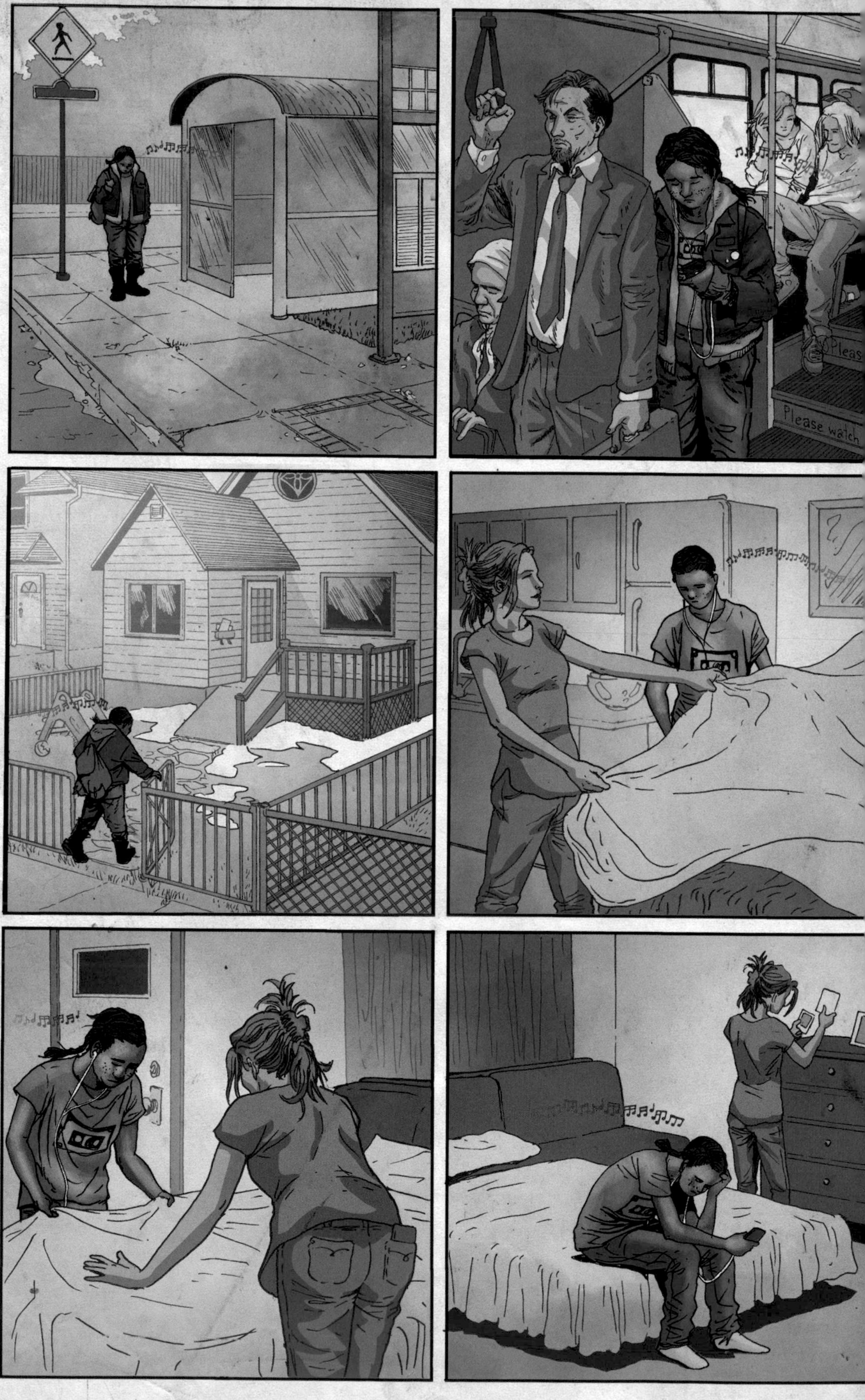
Pleas
Please watch

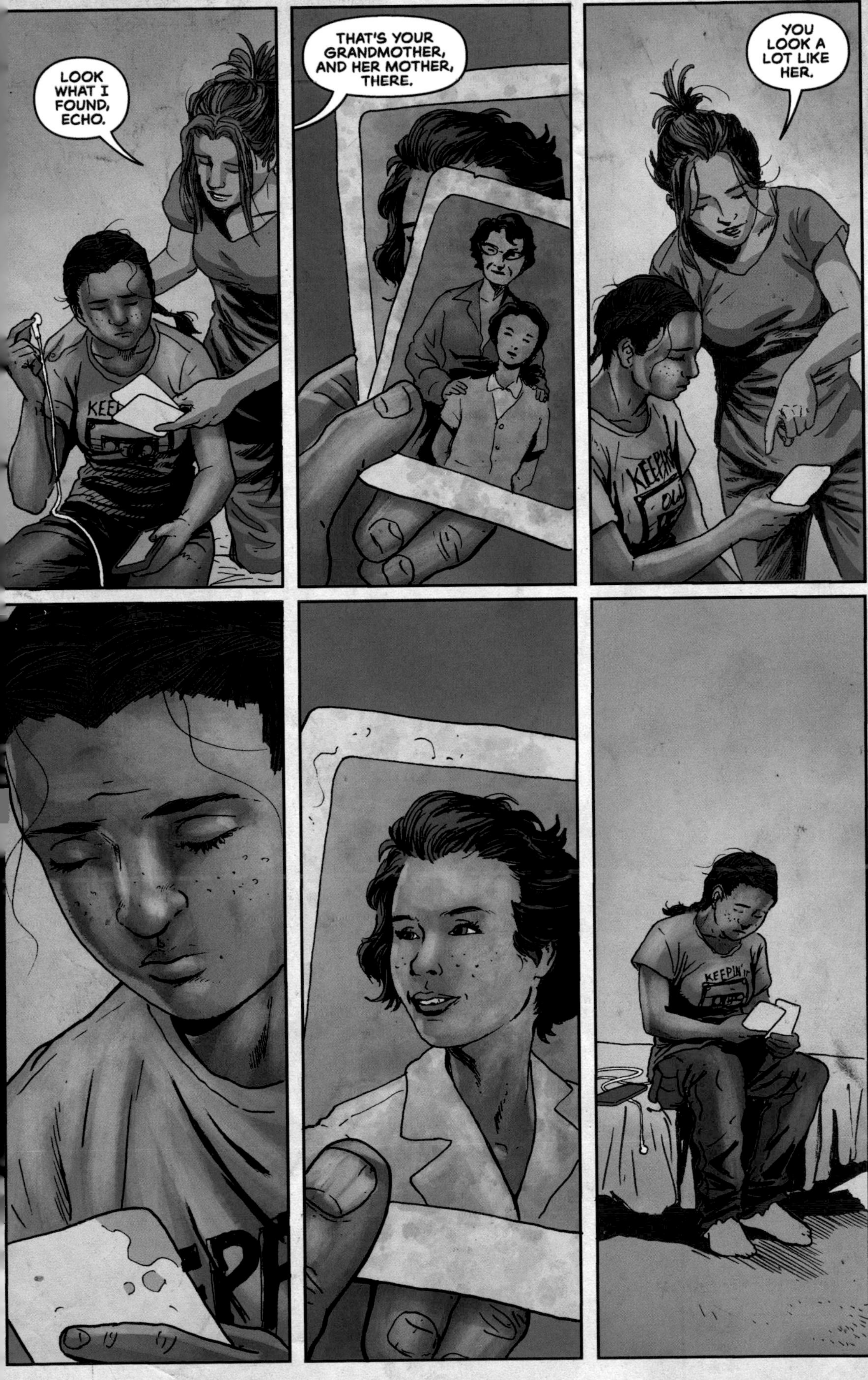
LOOK WHAT I FOUND, ECHO.
THAT'S YOUR GRANDMOTHER, AND HER MOTHER, THERE.
YOU LOOK A LOT LIKE HER.

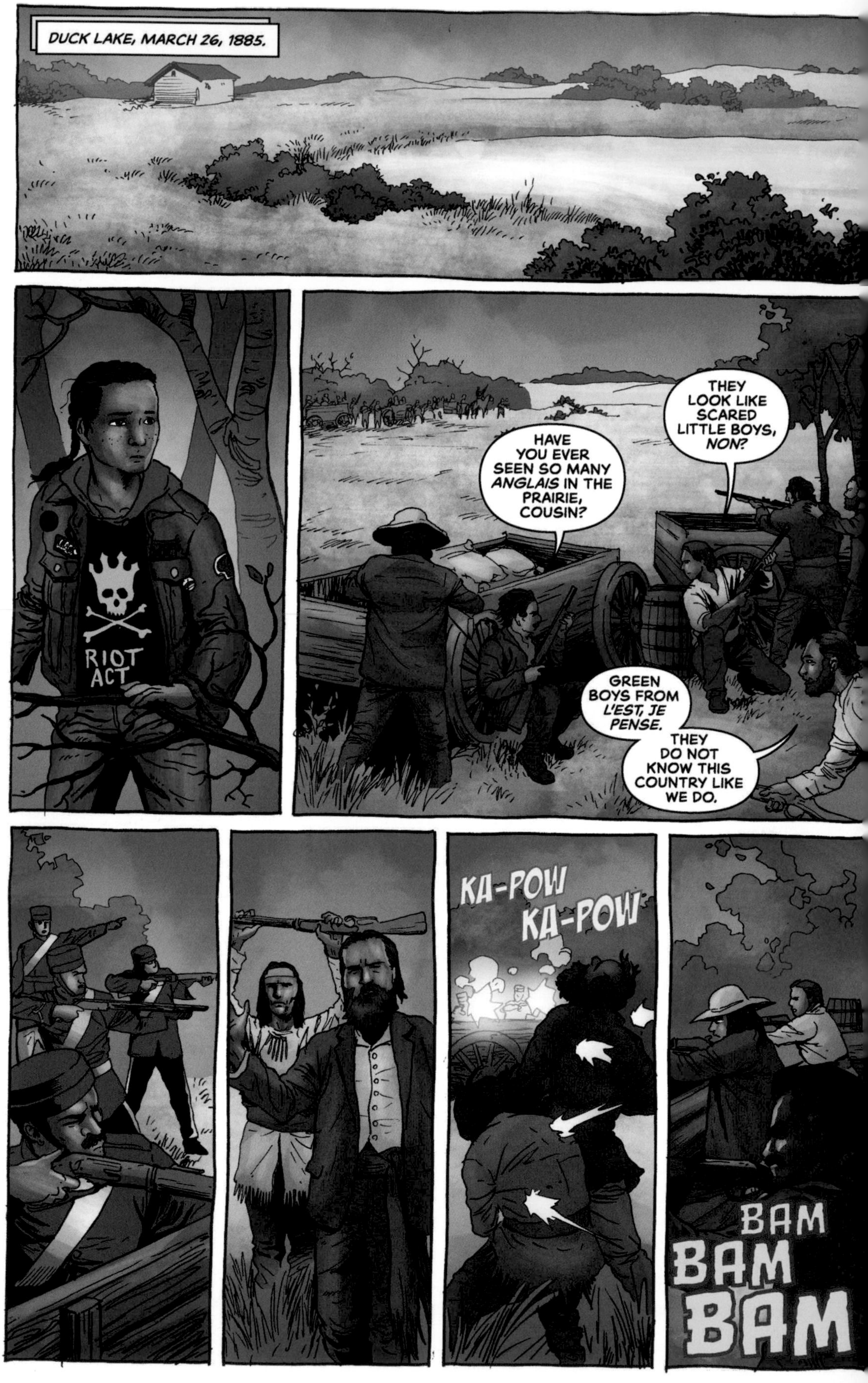
DUCK LAKE, MARCH 26, 1885.
RIOT ACT
HAVE YOU EVER SEEN SO MANY ANGLAIS IN THE PRAIRIE, COUSIN?
THEY LOOK LIKE SCARED LITTLE BOYS, NON?
GREEN BOYS FROM L'EST, JE PENSE.
THEY DO NOT KNOW THIS COUNTRY LIKE WE DO.
KA-POW
KA-POW
BAM
BAM
BAM

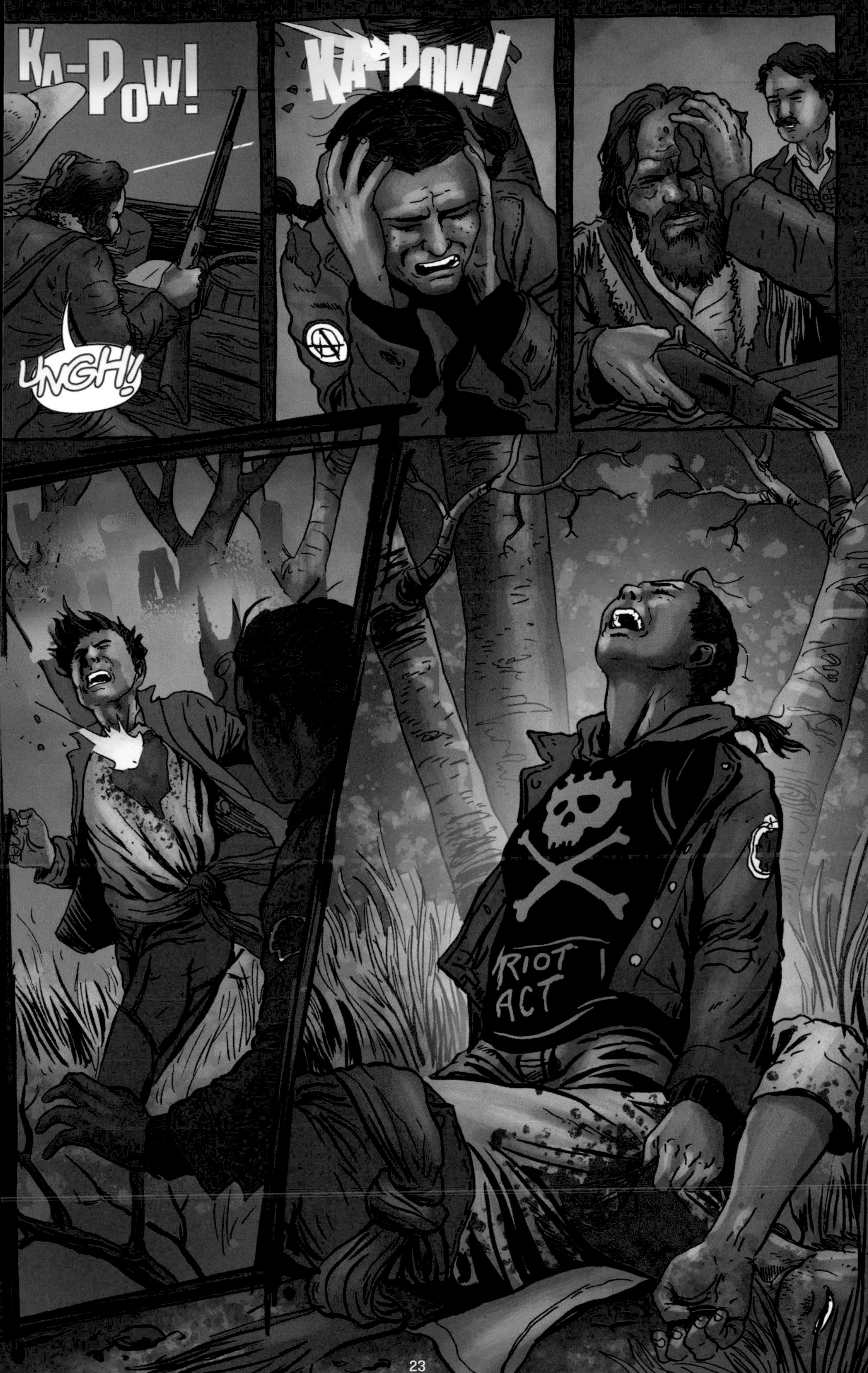

KA-POW!
UNGH!
KA-POW!
RIOT ACT

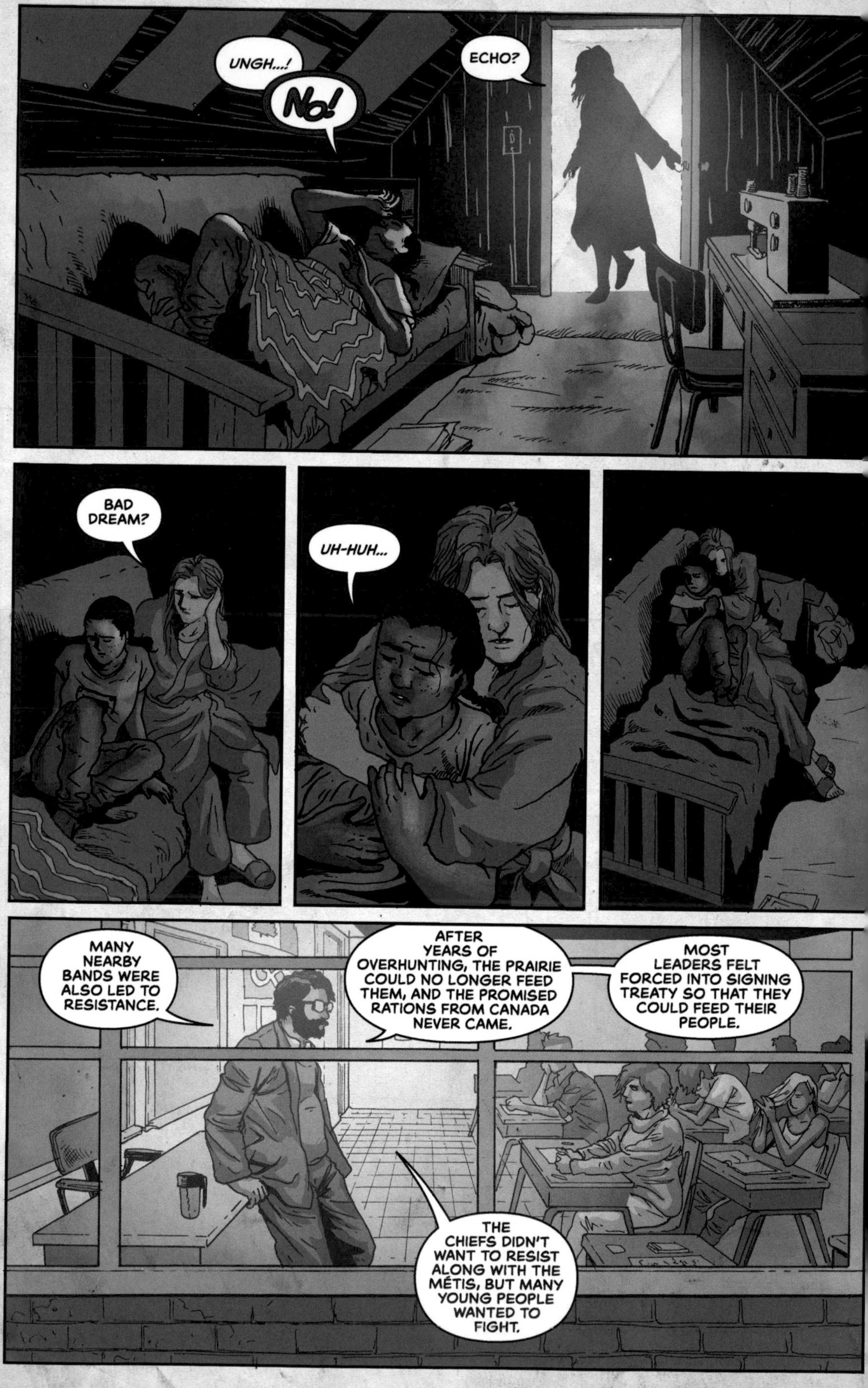
UNGH...!
No!
ECHO?
BAD DREAM?
UH-HUH...
MANY NEARBY BANDS WERE ALSO LED TO RESISTANCE.
AFTER YEARS OF OVERHUNTING, THE PRAIRIE COULD NO LONGER FEED THEM, AND THE PROMISED RATIONS FROM CANADA NEVER CAME.
MOST LEADERS FELT FORCED INTO SIGNING TREATY SO THAT THEY COULD FEED THEIR PEOPLE.
THE CHIEFS DIDN'T WANT TO RESIST ALONG WITH THE MÉTIS, BUT MANY YOUNG PEOPLE WANTED TO FIGHT.

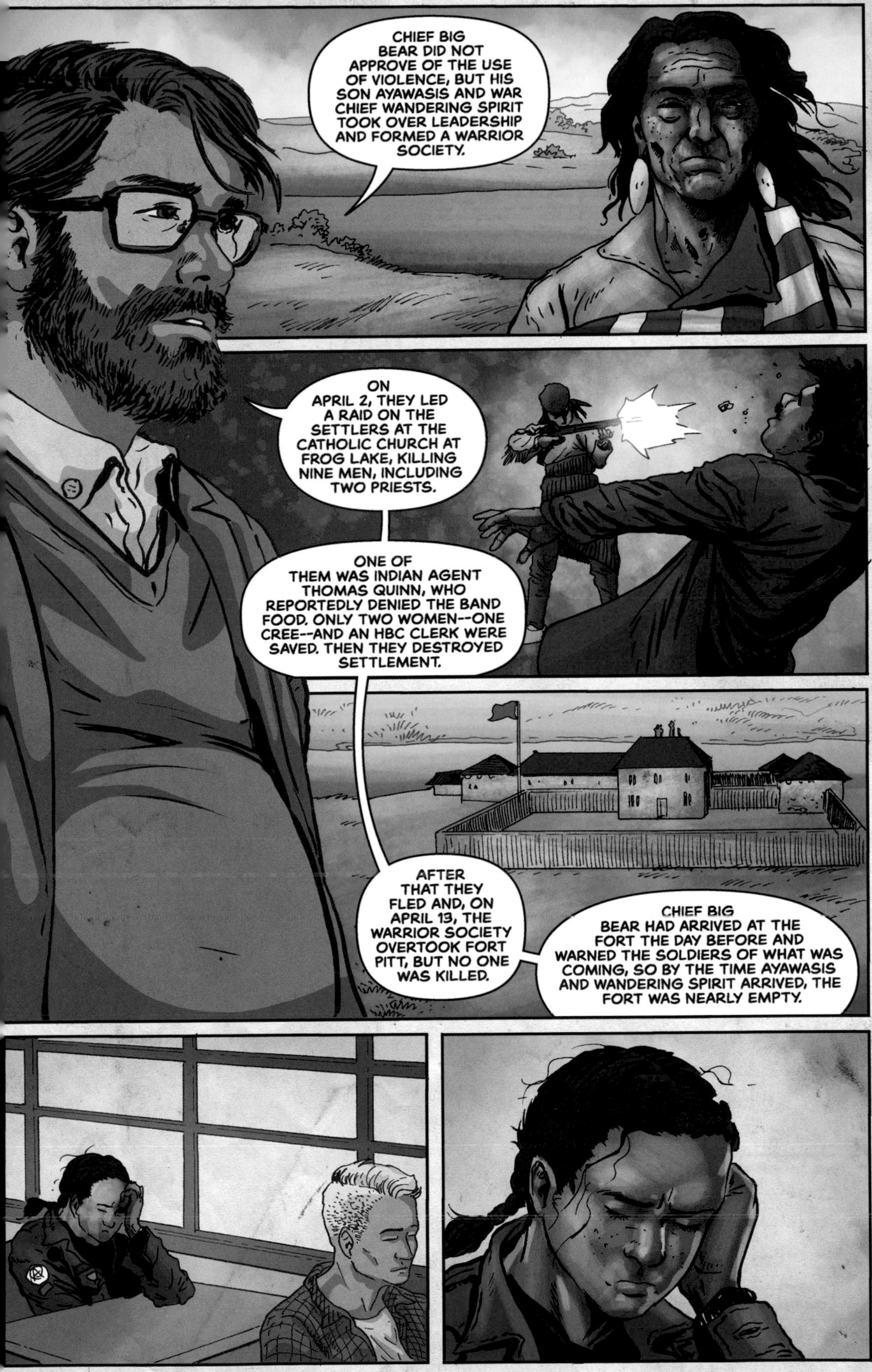
CHIEF BIG BEAR DID NOT APPROVE OF THE USE OF VIOLENCE, BUT HIS SON AYAWASIS AND WAR CHIEF WANDERING SPIRIT TOOK OVER LEADERSHIP AND FORMED A WARRIOR SOCIETY.
ON APRIL 2, THEY LED A RAID ON THE SETTLERS AT THE CATHOLIC CHURCH AT FROG LAKE, KILLING NINE MEN, INCLUDING TWO PRIESTS.
ONE OF THEM WAS INDIAN AGENT THOMAS QUINN, WHO REPORTEDLY DENIED THE BAND FOOD. ONLY TWO WOMEN--ONE CREE--AND AN HBC CLERK WERE SAVED. THEN THEY DESTROYED SETTLEMENT.
AFTER THAT THEY FLED AND, ON APRIL 13, THE WARRIOR SOCIETY OVERTOOK FORT PITT, BUT NO ONE WAS KILLED.
CHIEF BIG BEAR HAD ARRIVED AT THE FORT THE DAY BEFORE AND WARNED THE SOLDIERS OF WHAT WAS COMING, SO BY THE TIME AYAWASIS AND WANDERING SPIRIT ARRIVED, THE FORT WAS NEARLY EMPTY.

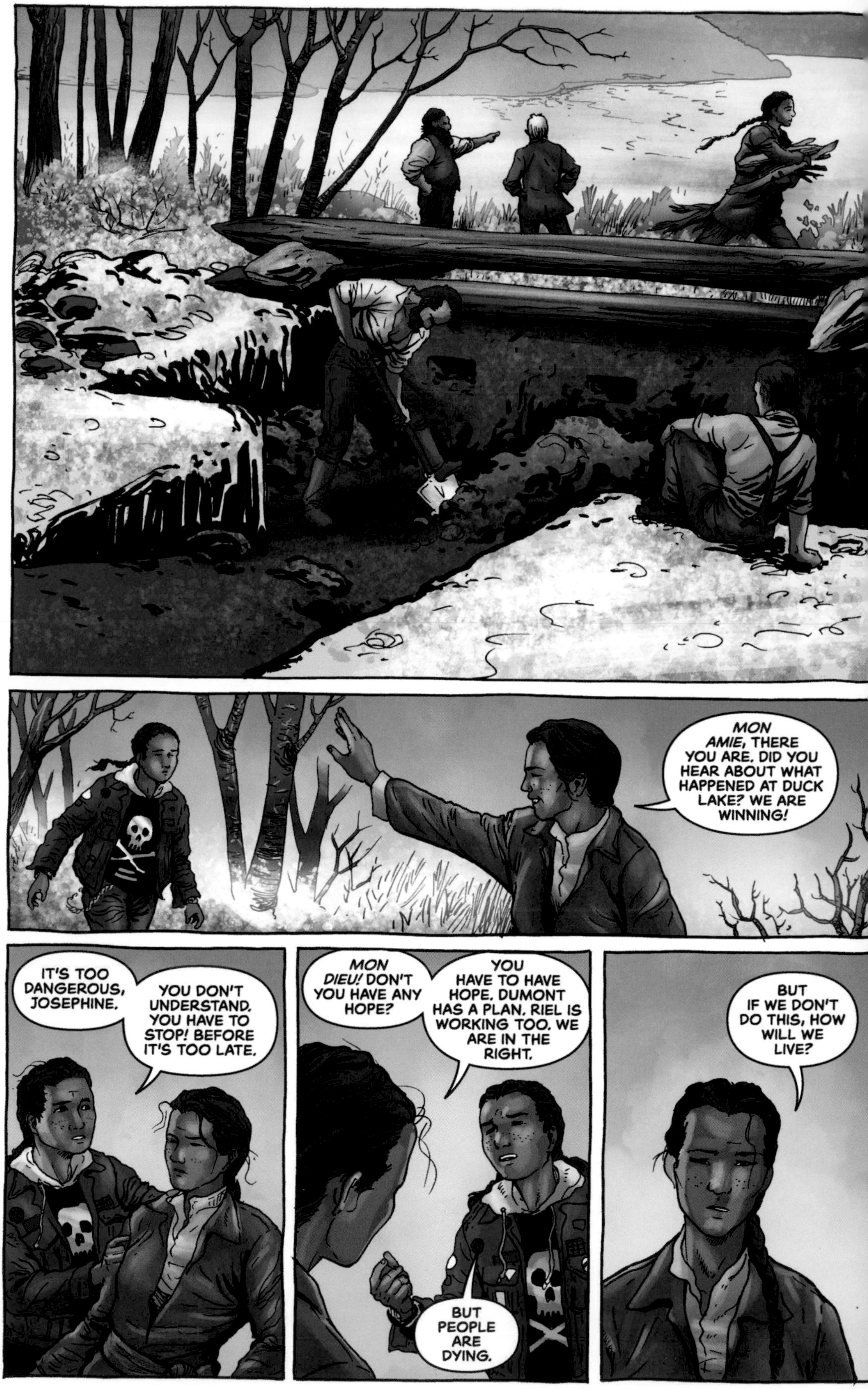
MON AMIE, THERE YOU ARE. DID YOU HEAR ABOUT WHAT HAPPENED AT DUCK LAKE? WE ARE WINNING!
IT'S TOO DANGEROUS, JOSEPHINE.
YOU DON'T UNDERSTAND. YOU HAVE TO *STOP!* BEFORE IT'S TOO LATE.
MON DIEU! DON'T YOU HAVE ANY HOPE?
YOU HAVE TO HAVE HOPE. DUMONT HAS A PLAN. RIEL IS WORKING TOO. WE ARE IN THE RIGHT.
BUT PEOPLE ARE DYING.
BUT IF WE DON'T DO THIS, HOW WILL WE LIVE?

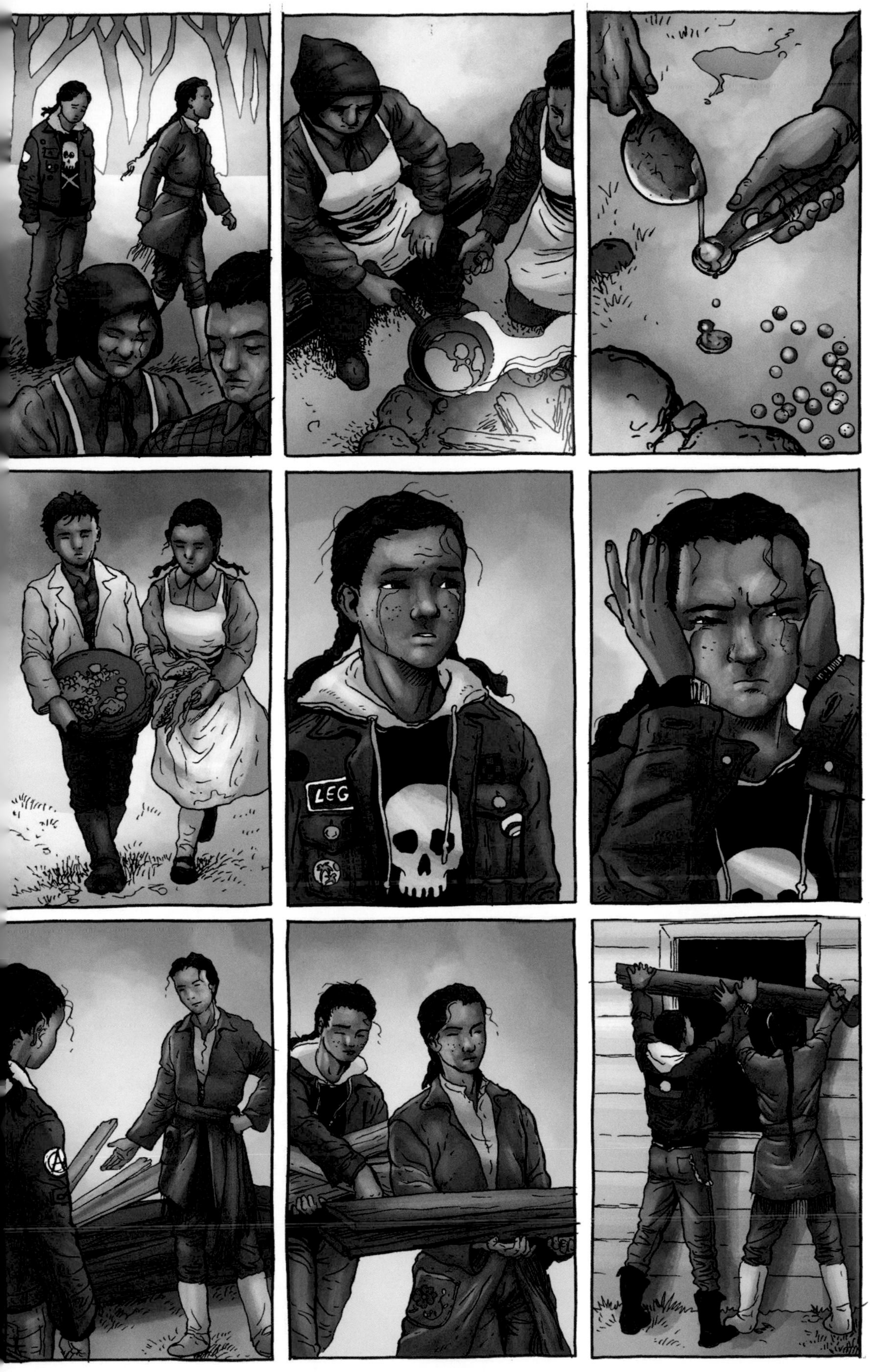
LEG

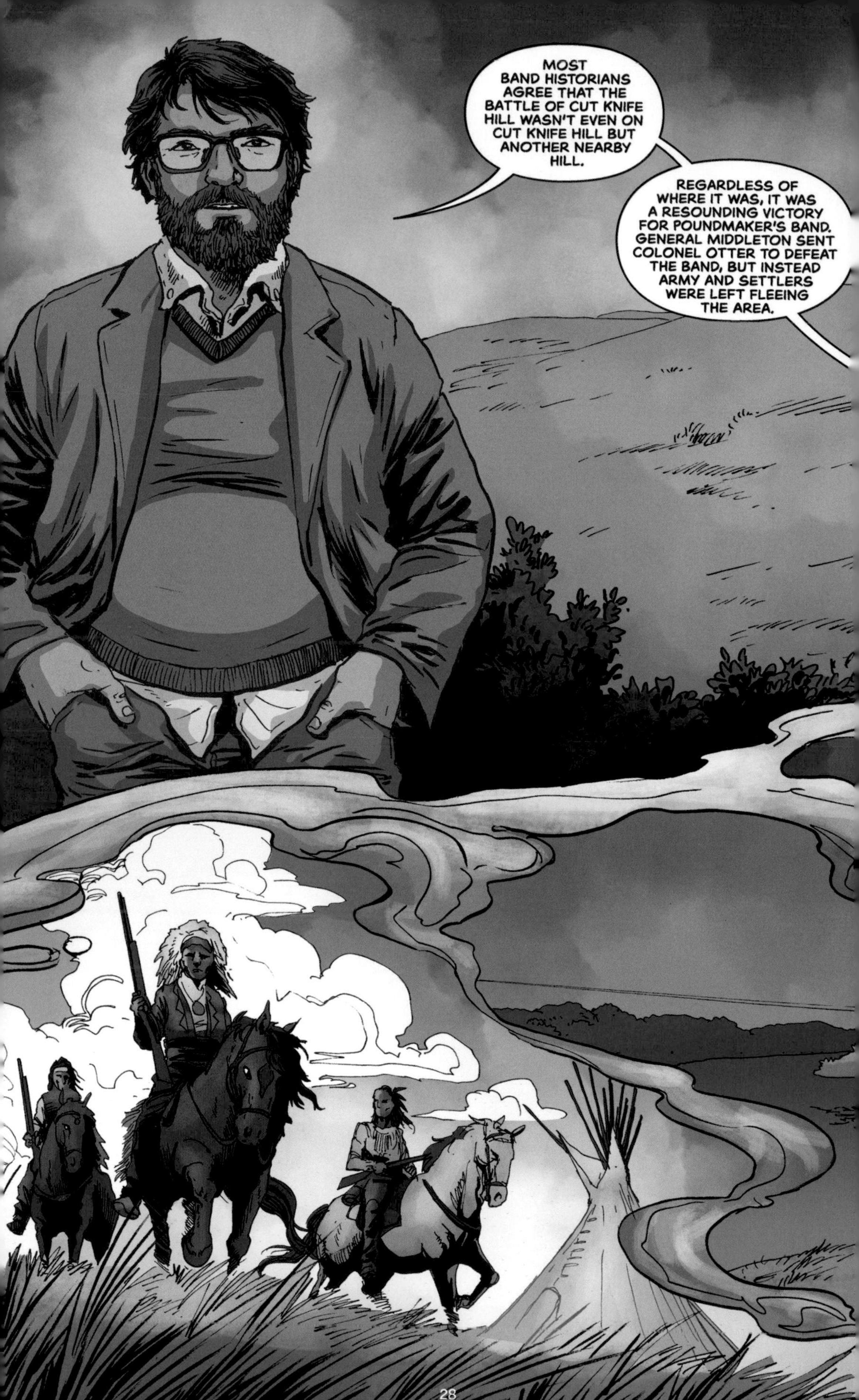
MOST BAND HISTORIANS AGREE THAT THE BATTLE OF CUT KNIFE HILL WASN'T EVEN ON CUT KNIFE HILL BUT ANOTHER NEARBY HILL.
REGARDLESS OF WHERE IT WAS, IT WAS A RESOUNDING VICTORY FOR POUNDMAKER'S BAND. GENERAL MIDDLETON SENT COLONEL OTTER TO DEFEAT THE BAND, BUT INSTEAD ARMY AND SETTLERS WERE LEFT FLEEING THE AREA.

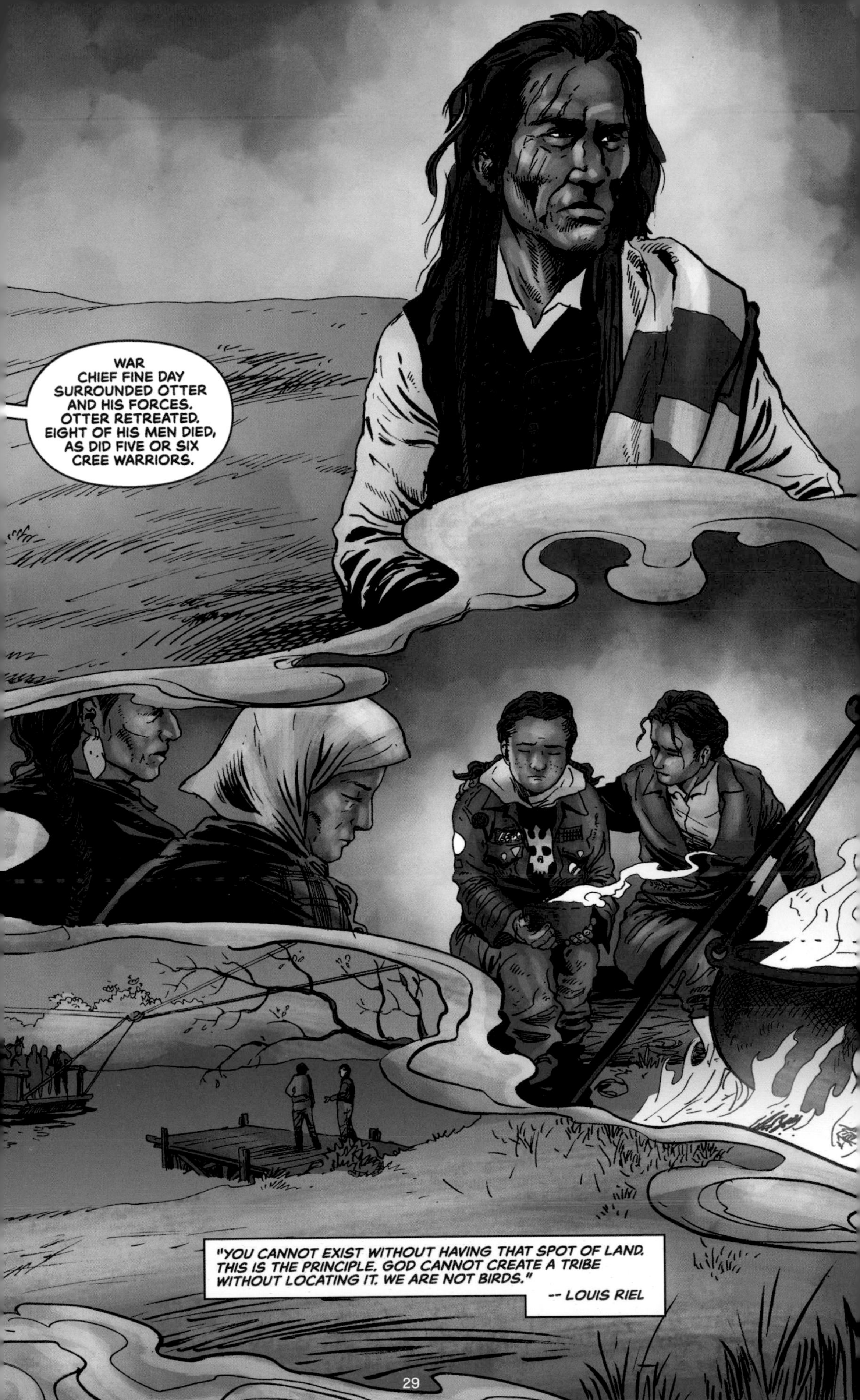
WAR CHIEF FINE DAY SURROUNDED OTTER AND HIS FORCES. OTTER RETREATED. EIGHT OF HIS MEN DIED, AS DID FIVE OR SIX CREE WARRIORS.
"YOU CANNOT EXIST WITHOUT HAVING THAT SPOT OF LAND. THIS IS THE PRINCIPLE. GOD CANNOT CREATE A TRIBE WITHOUT LOCATING IT. WE ARE NOT BIRDS."
-- LOUIS RIEL

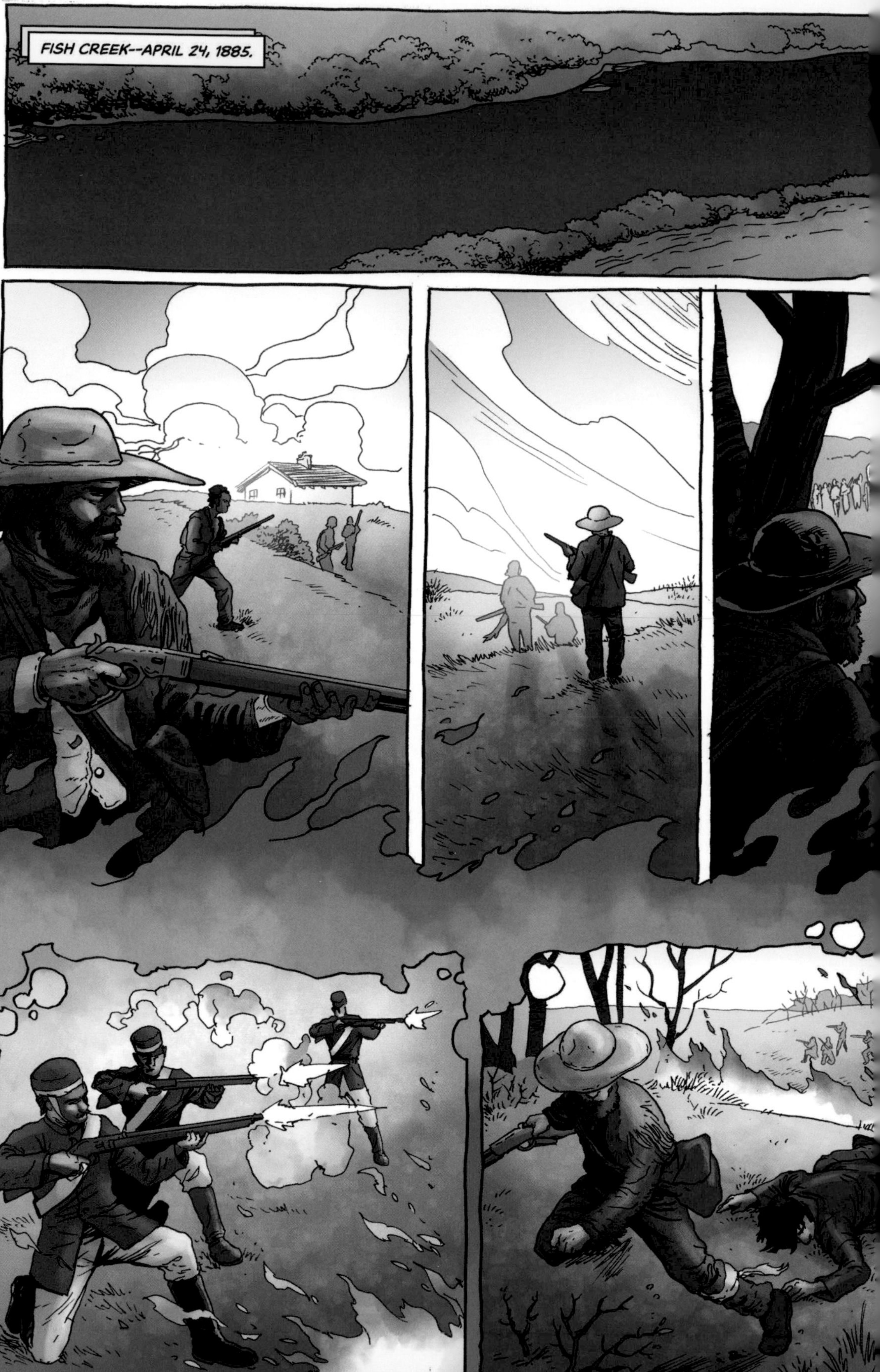
FISH CREEK--APRIL 24, 1885.

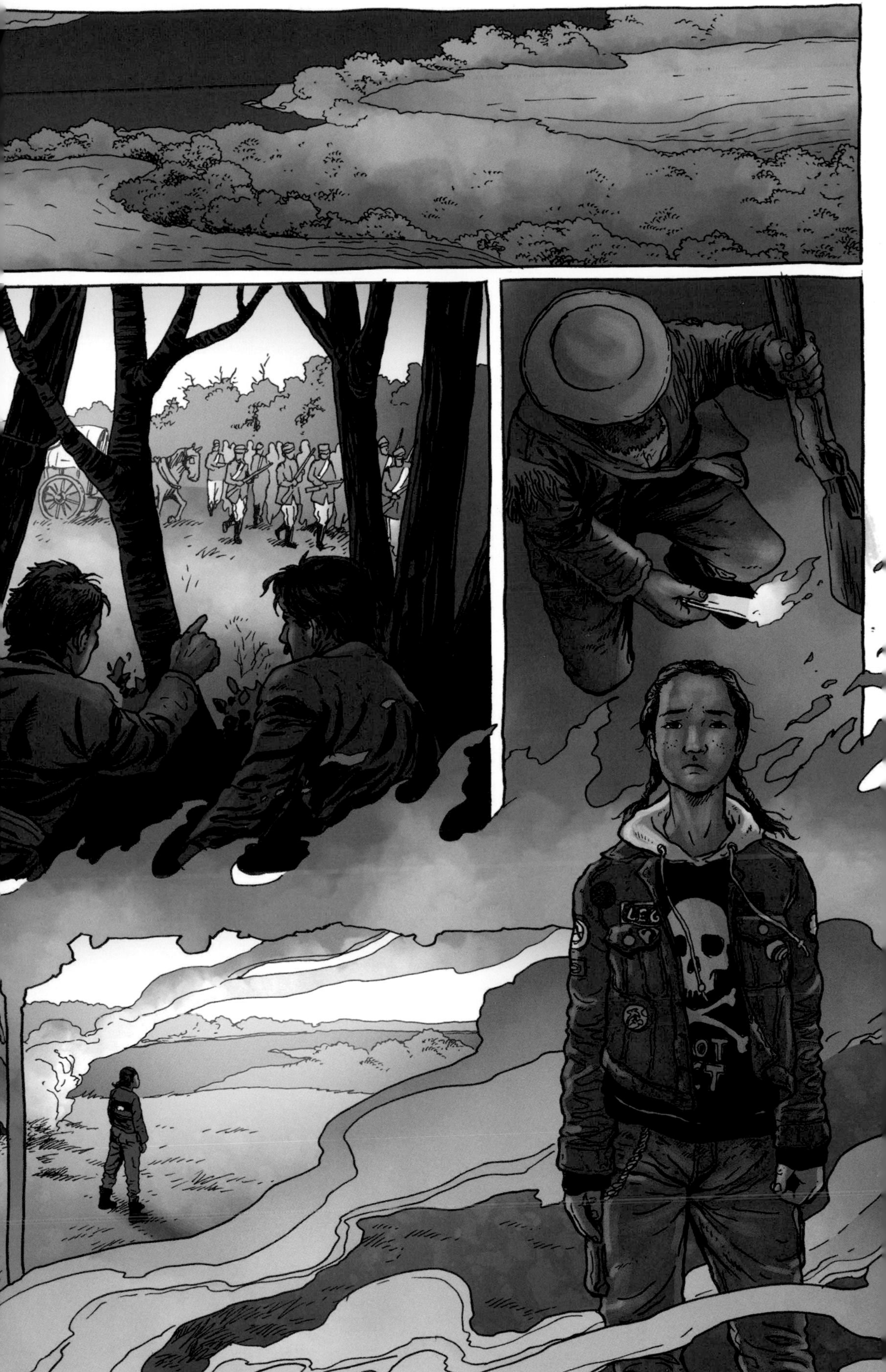

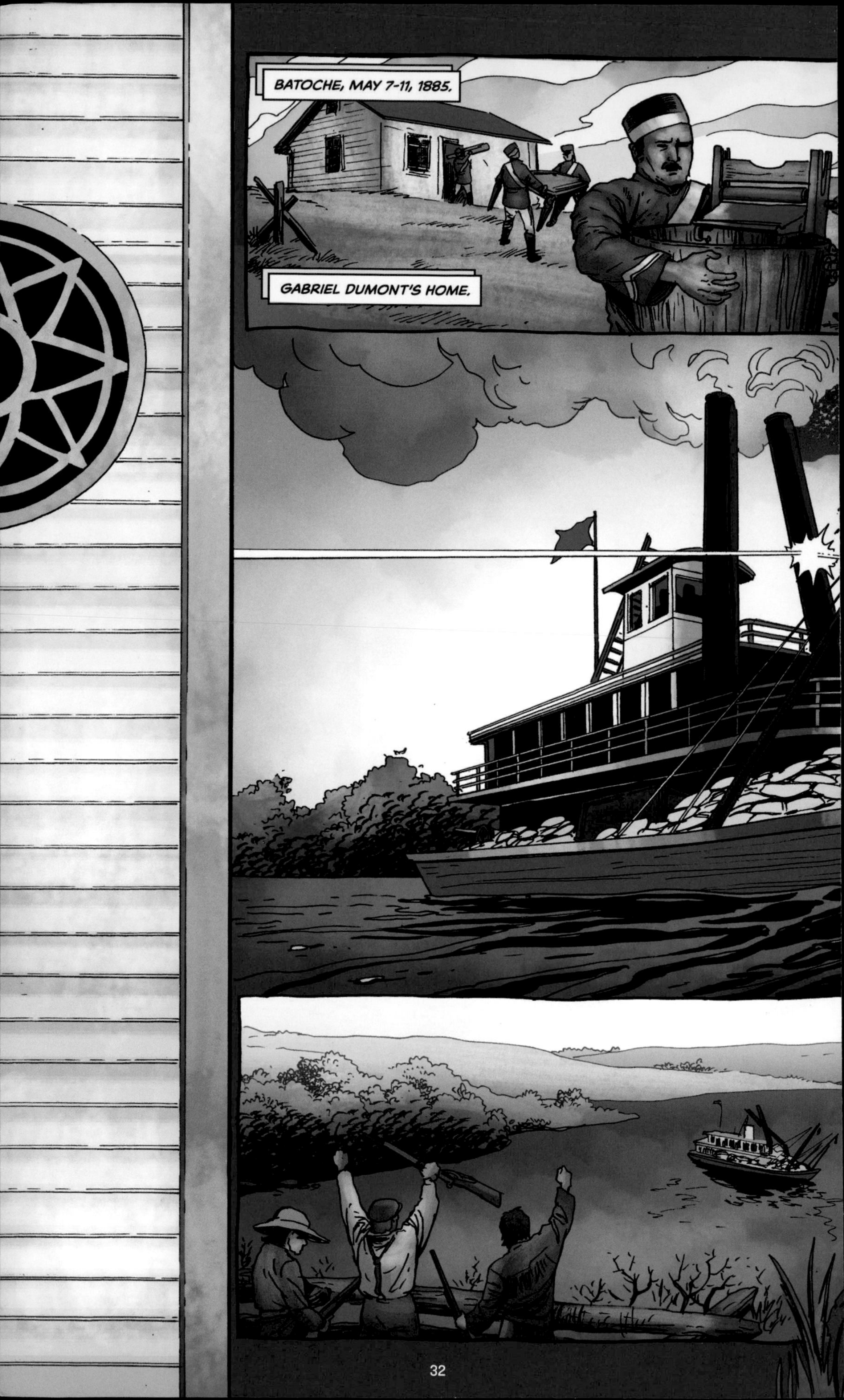
BATOCHE, MAY 7-11, 1885.
GABRIEL DUMONT'S HOME.

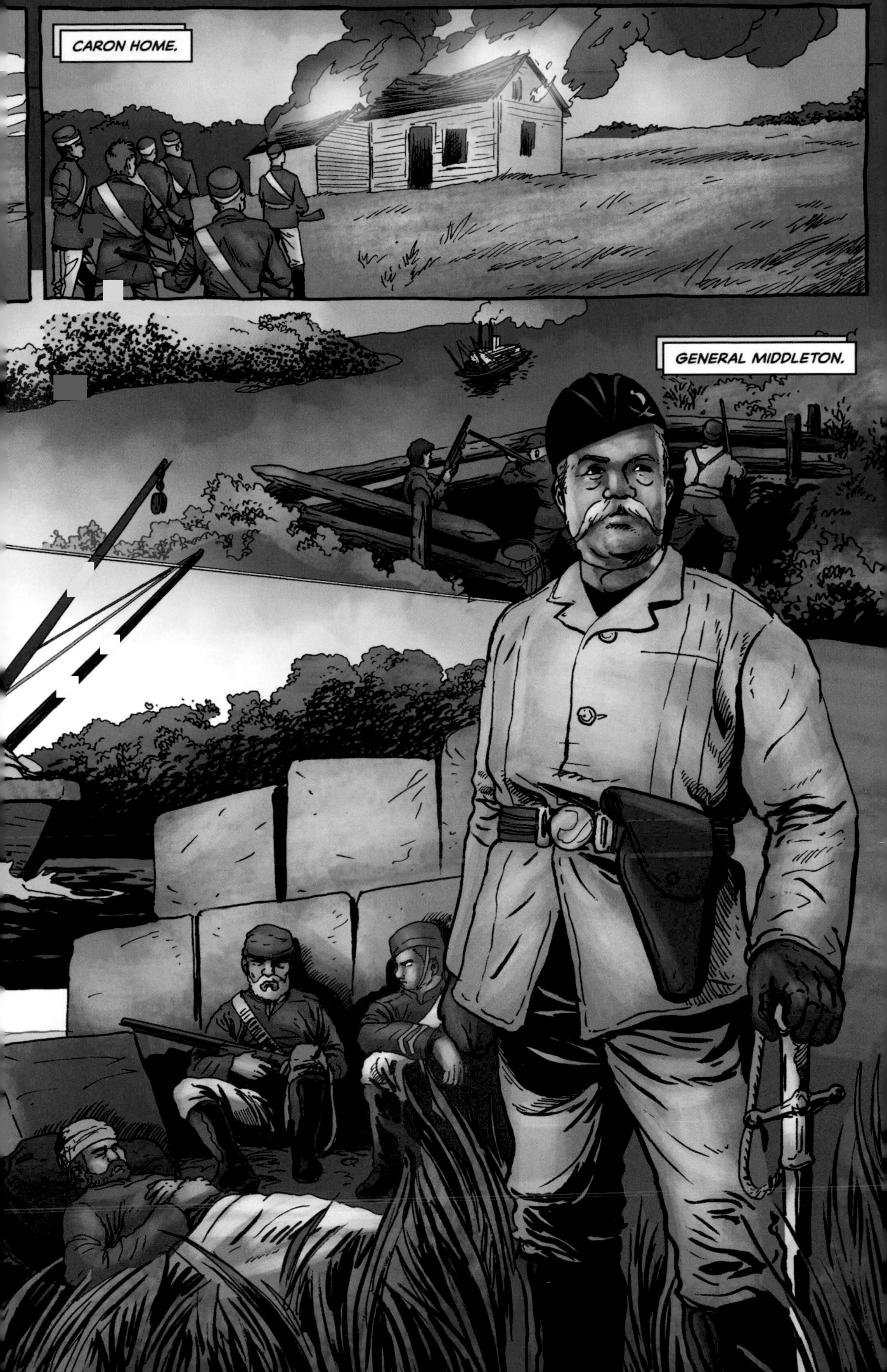
CARON HOME.
GENERAL MIDDLETON.

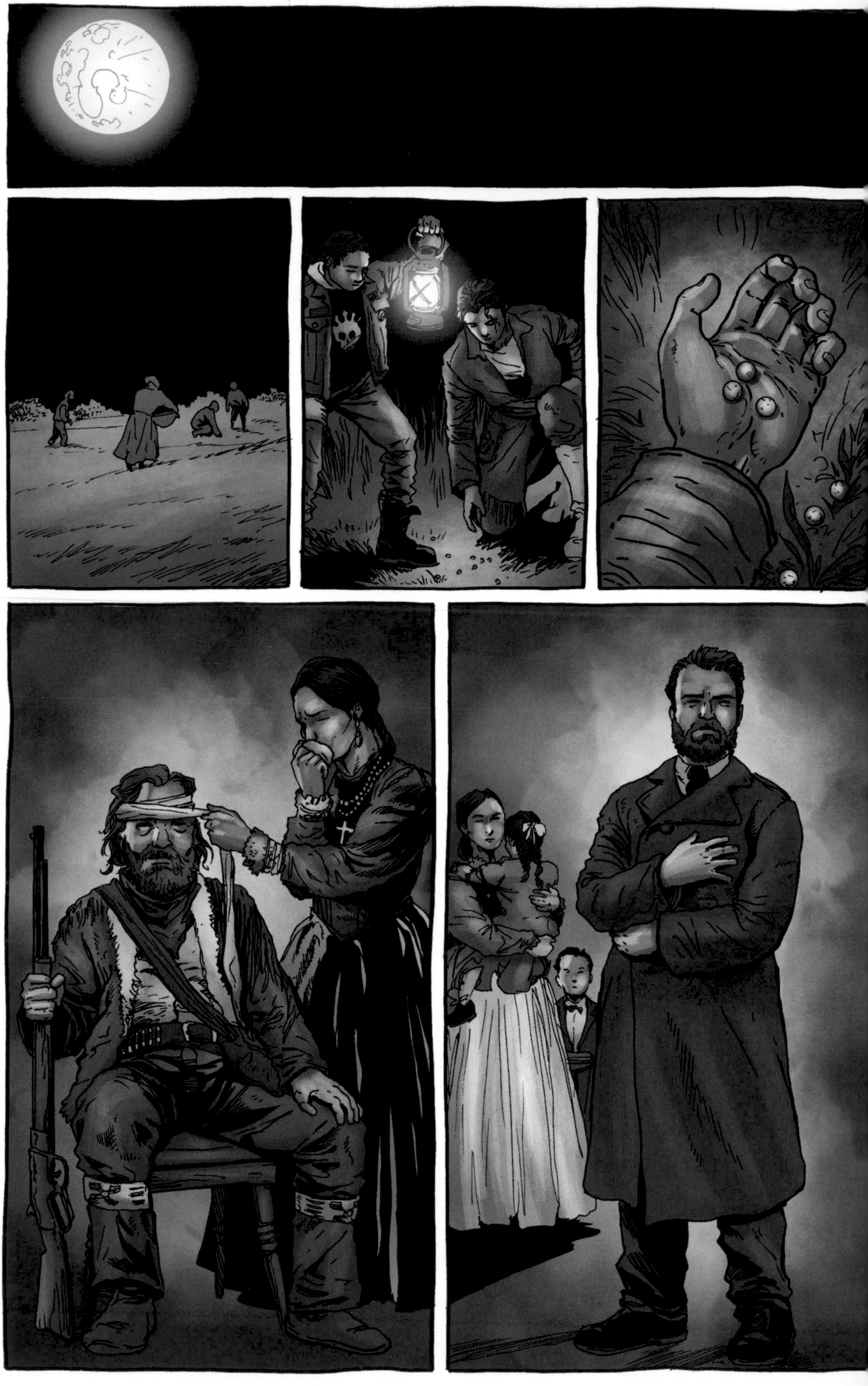

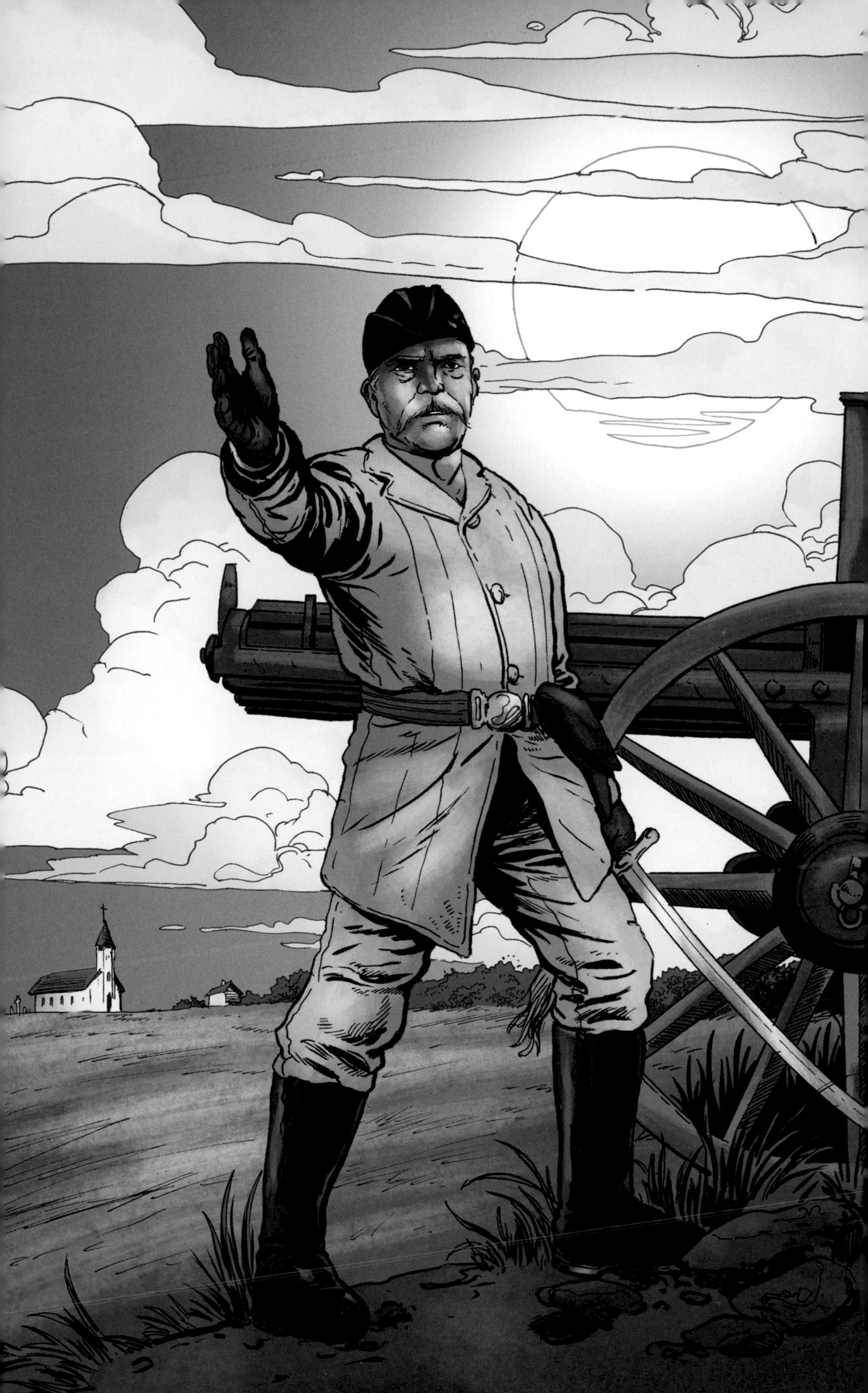

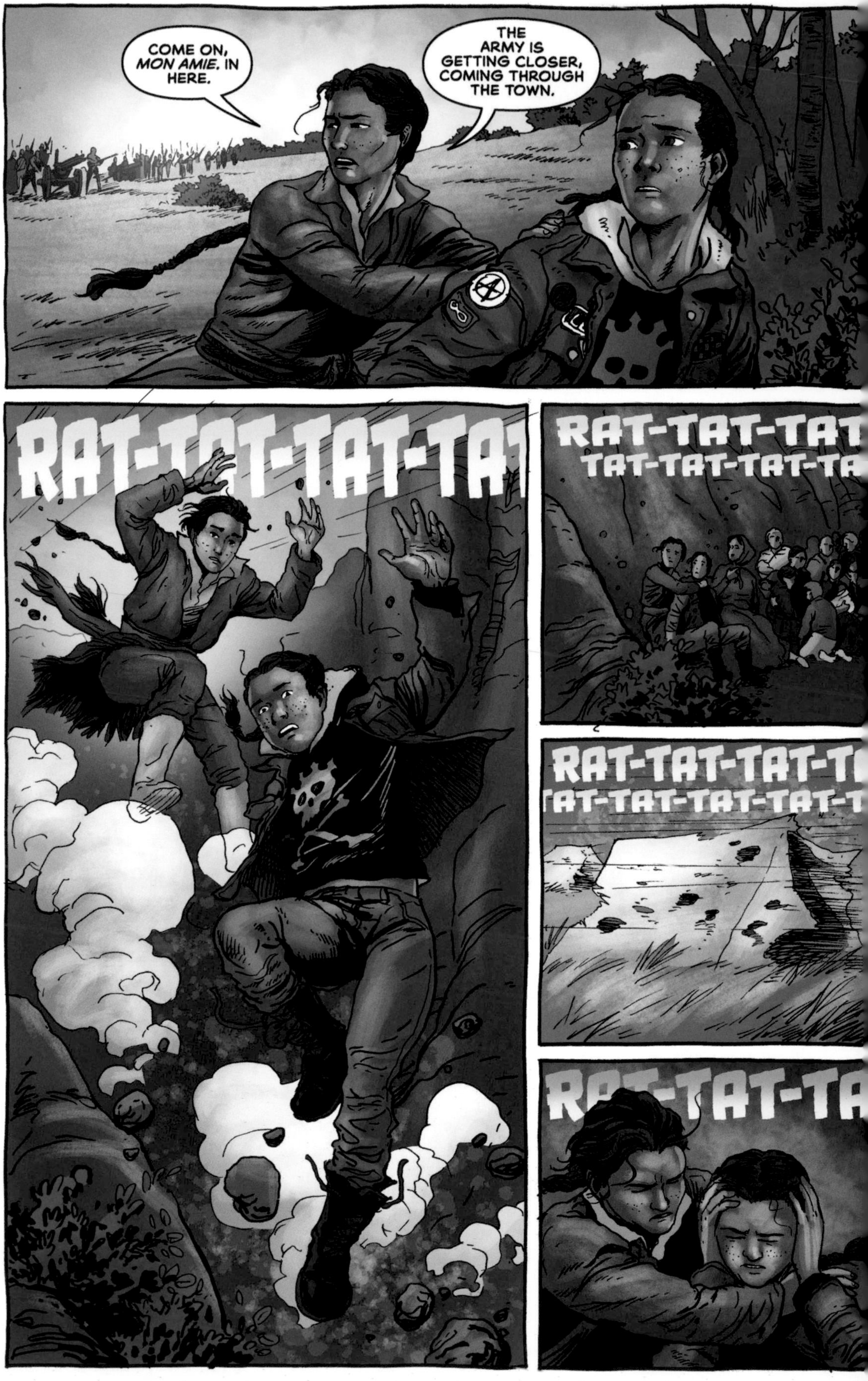
COME ON, *MON AMIE.* IN HERE.
THE ARMY IS GETTING CLOSER, COMING THROUGH THE TOWN.
RAT-TAT-TAT-TA
RAT-TAT-TAT
TAT-TAT-TAT-TA
RAT-TAT-TAT-T
TAT-TAT-TAT-TAT-
RAT-TAT-TA

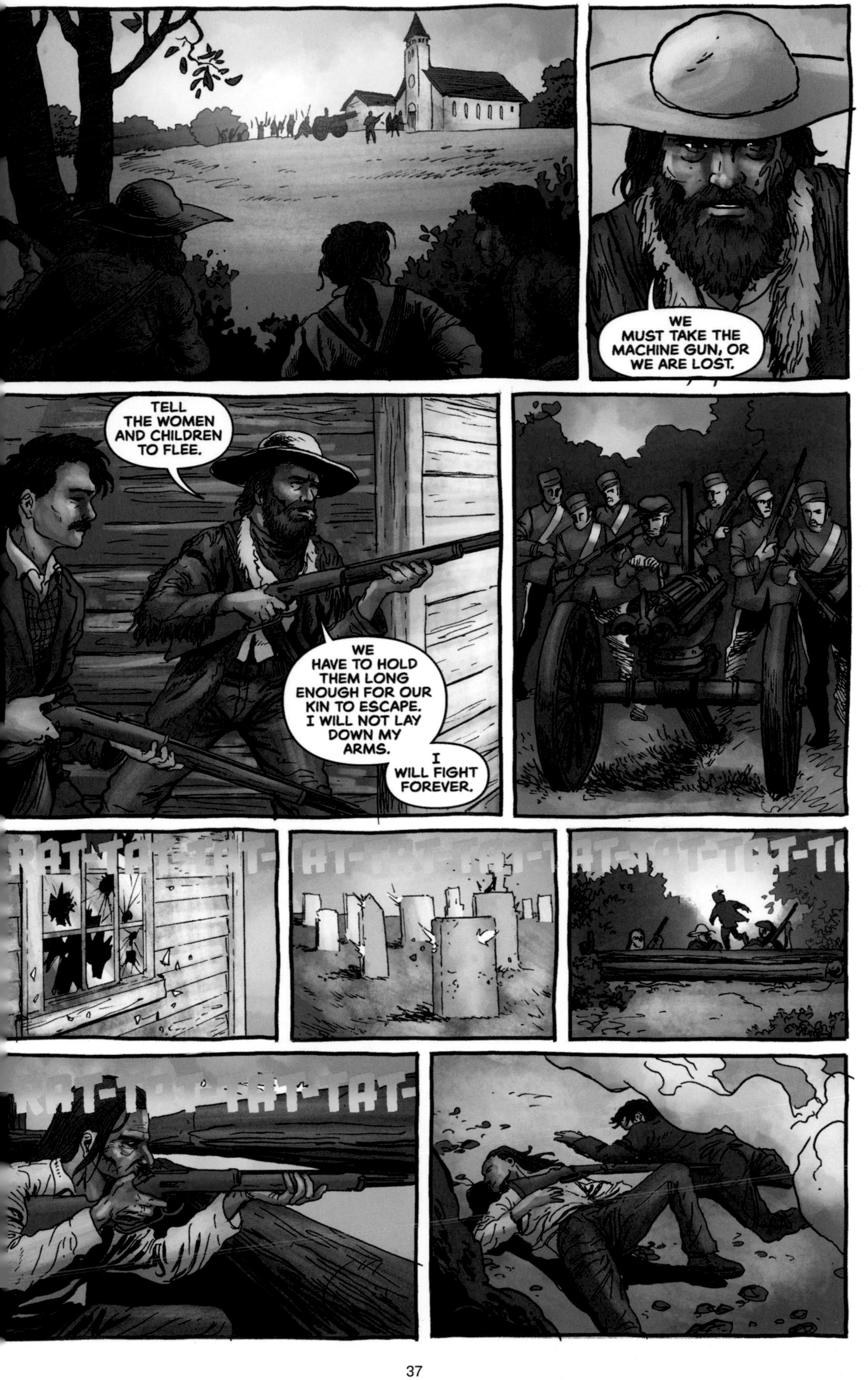
WE MUST TAKE THE MACHINE GUN, OR WE ARE LOST.
TELL THE WOMEN AND CHILDREN TO FLEE.
WE HAVE TO HOLD THEM LONG ENOUGH FOR OUR KIN TO ESCAPE. I WILL NOT LAY DOWN MY ARMS.
I WILL FIGHT FOREVER.
RAT-TAT-TAT-
TAT-TAT-TAT-T
AT-TAT-TAT-T
RAT-TAT-TAT-TAT-

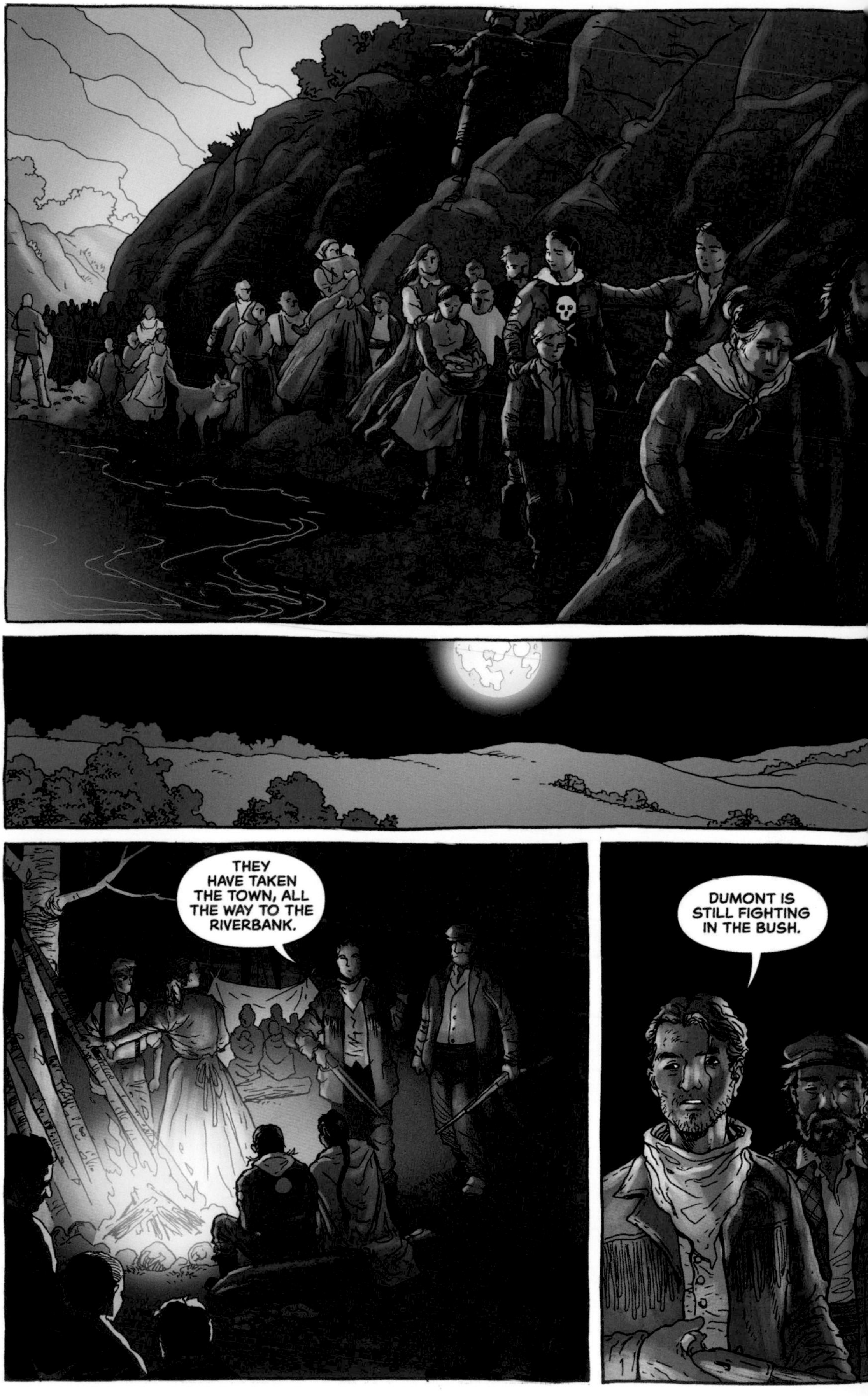
THEY HAVE TAKEN THE TOWN, ALL THE WAY TO THE RIVERBANK.
DUMONT IS STILL FIGHTING IN THE BUSH.

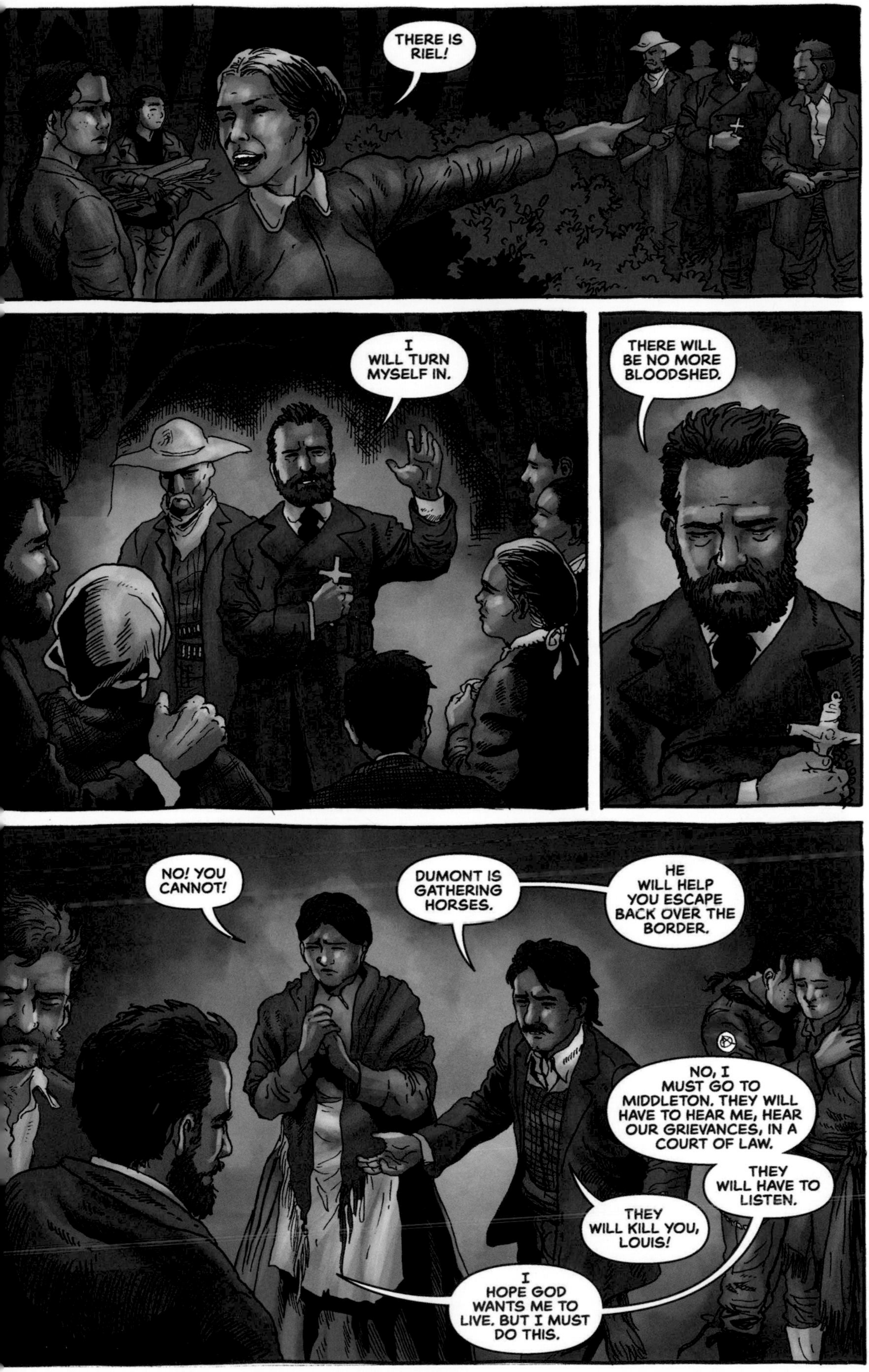
THERE IS RIEL!
I WILL TURN MYSELF IN.
THERE WILL BE NO MORE BLOODSHED.
NO! YOU CANNOT!
DUMONT IS GATHERING HORSES.
HE WILL HELP YOU ESCAPE BACK OVER THE BORDER.
NO, I MUST GO TO MIDDLETON. THEY WILL HAVE TO HEAR ME, HEAR OUR GRIEVANCES, IN A COURT OF LAW.
THEY WILL HAVE TO LISTEN.
THEY WILL KILL YOU, LOUIS!
I HOPE GOD WANTS ME TO LIVE. BUT I MUST DO THIS.

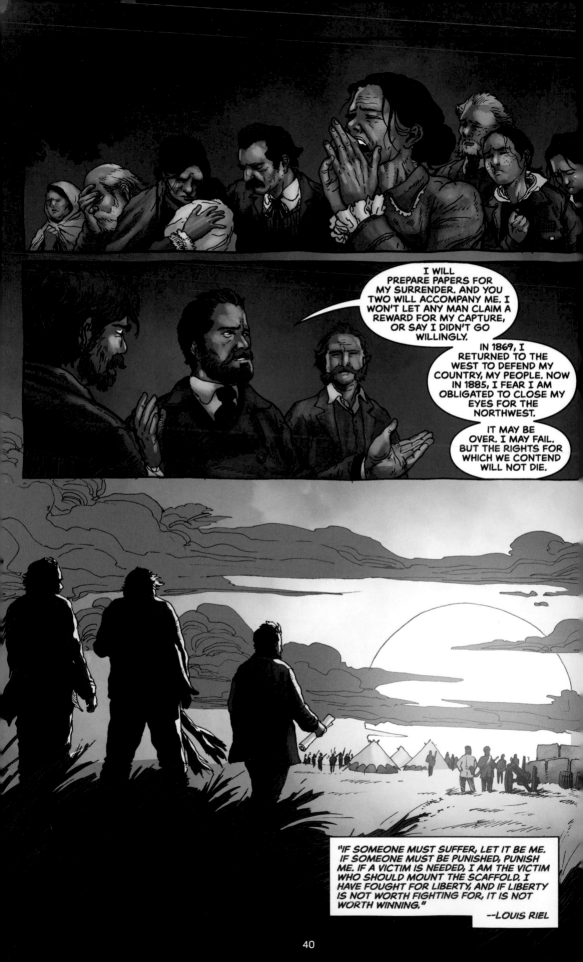

I WILL PREPARE PAPERS FOR MY SURRENDER. AND YOU TWO WILL ACCOMPANY ME. I WON'T LET ANY MAN CLAIM A REWARD FOR MY CAPTURE, OR SAY I DIDN'T GO WILLINGLY.

IN 1869, I RETURNED TO THE WEST TO DEFEND MY COUNTRY, MY PEOPLE. NOW IN 1885, I FEAR I AM OBLIGATED TO CLOSE MY EYES FOR THE NORTHWEST.

IT MAY BE OVER. I MAY FAIL. BUT THE RIGHTS FOR WHICH WE CONTEND WILL NOT DIE.

"IF SOMEONE MUST SUFFER, LET IT BE ME. IF SOMEONE MUST BE PUNISHED, PUNISH ME. IF A VICTIM IS NEEDED, I AM THE VICTIM WHO SHOULD MOUNT THE SCAFFOLD. I HAVE FOUGHT FOR LIBERTY, AND IF LIBERTY IS NOT WORTH FIGHTING FOR, IT IS NOT WORTH WINNING."

--LOUIS RIEL

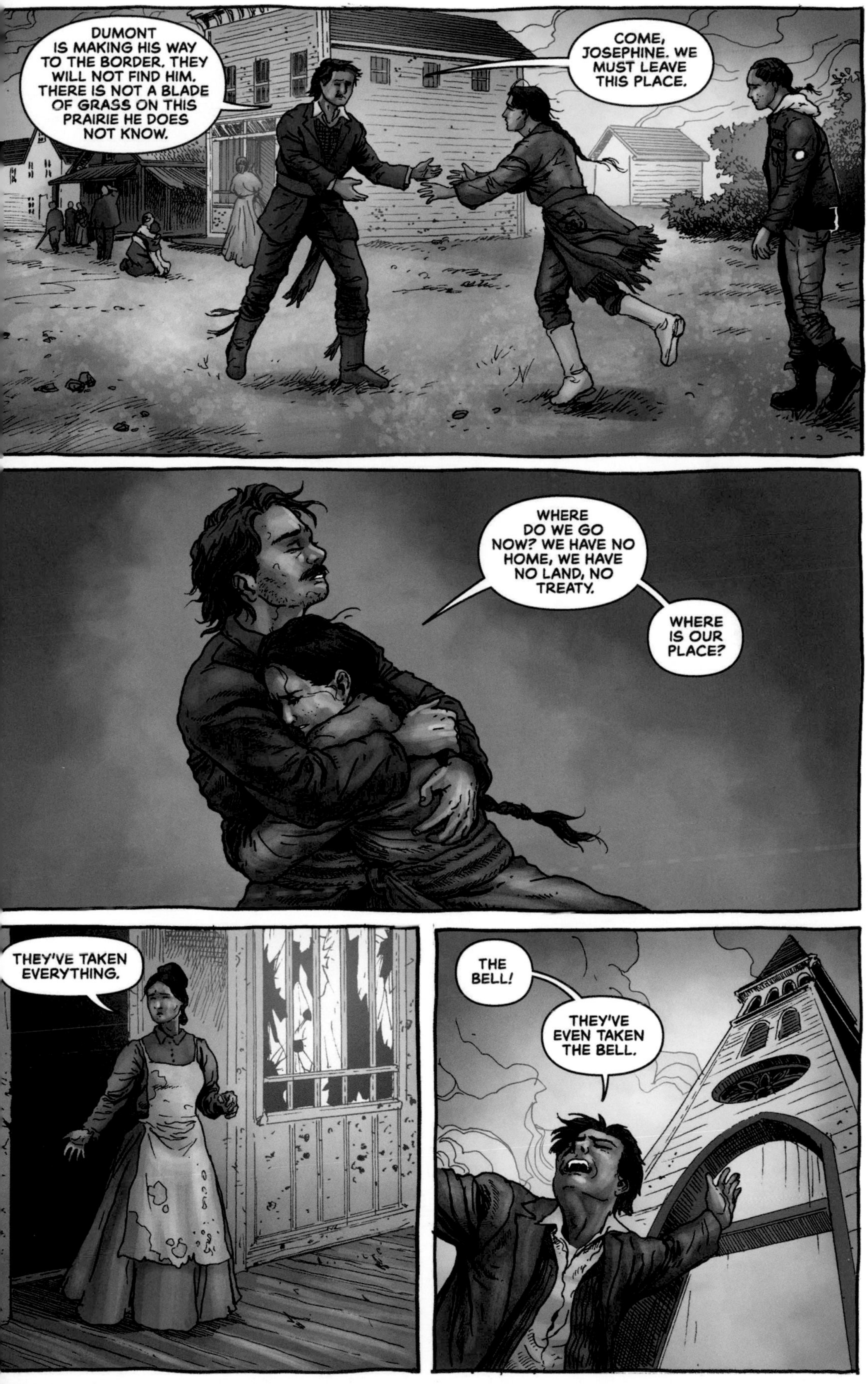
DUMONT IS MAKING HIS WAY TO THE BORDER. THEY WILL NOT FIND HIM. THERE IS NOT A BLADE OF GRASS ON THIS PRAIRIE HE DOES NOT KNOW.
COME, JOSEPHINE. WE MUST LEAVE THIS PLACE.
WHERE DO WE GO NOW? WE HAVE NO HOME, WE HAVE NO LAND, NO TREATY.
WHERE IS OUR PLACE?
THEY'VE TAKEN EVERYTHING.
THE BELL!
THEY'VE EVEN TAKEN THE BELL.

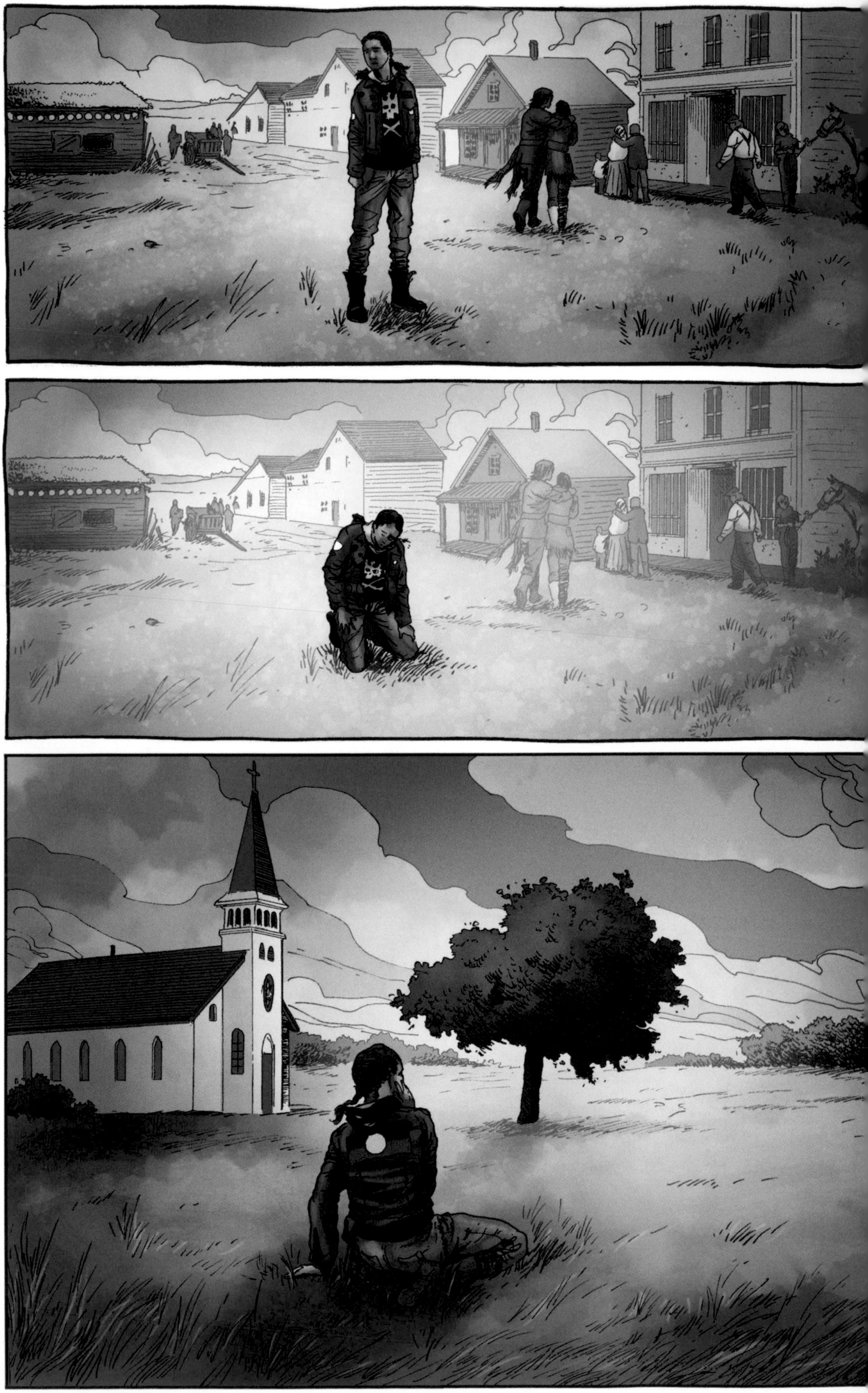

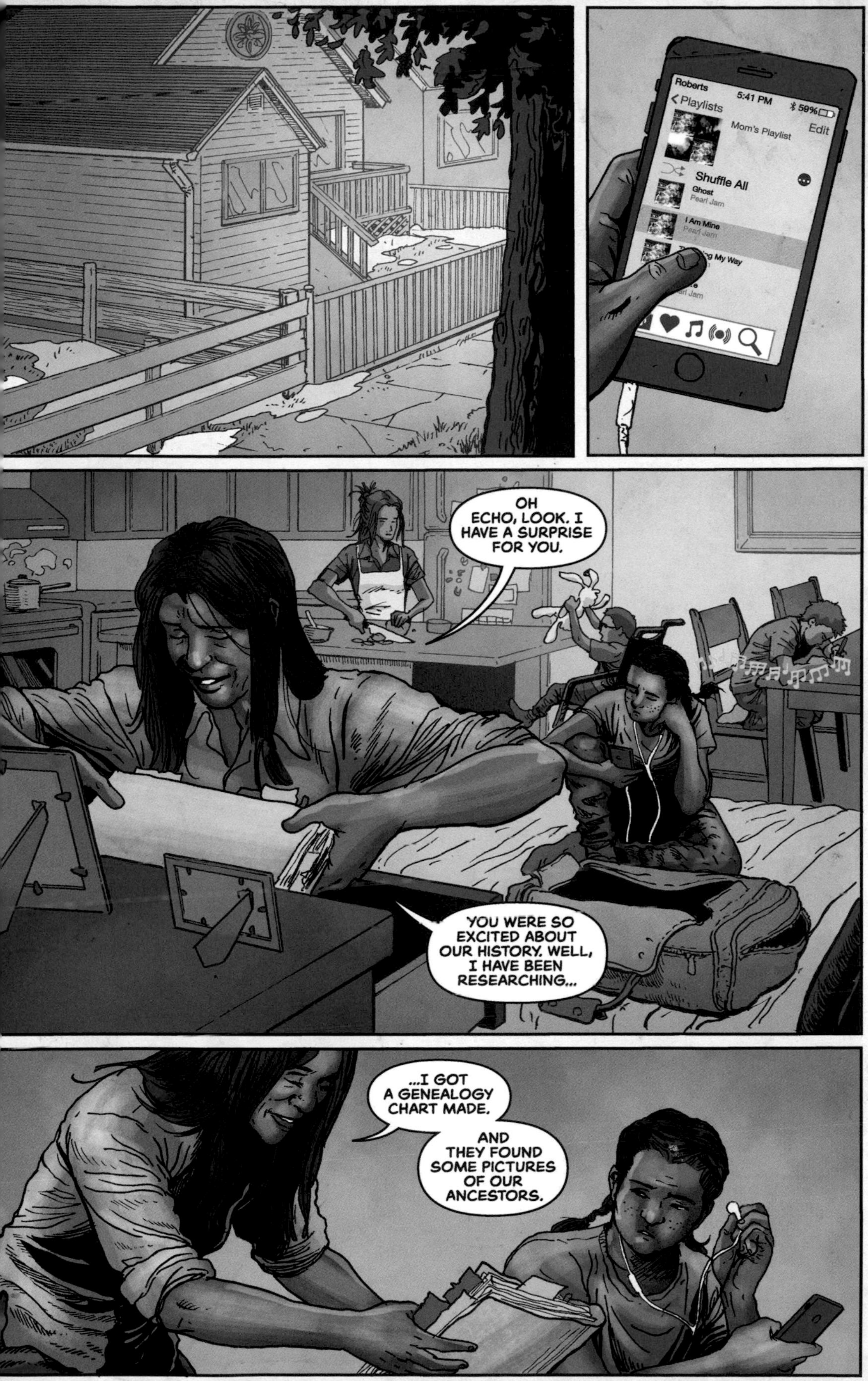
Roberts
5:41 PM
59%
Playlists
Mom's Playlist
Edit
Shuffle All
Ghost
Pearl Jam
I Am Mine
Pearl Jam
OH ECHO, LOOK. I HAVE A SURPRISE FOR YOU.
YOU WERE SO EXCITED ABOUT OUR HISTORY. WELL, I HAVE BEEN RESEARCHING...
...I GOT A GENEALOGY CHART MADE.
AND THEY FOUND SOME PICTURES OF OUR ANCESTORS.

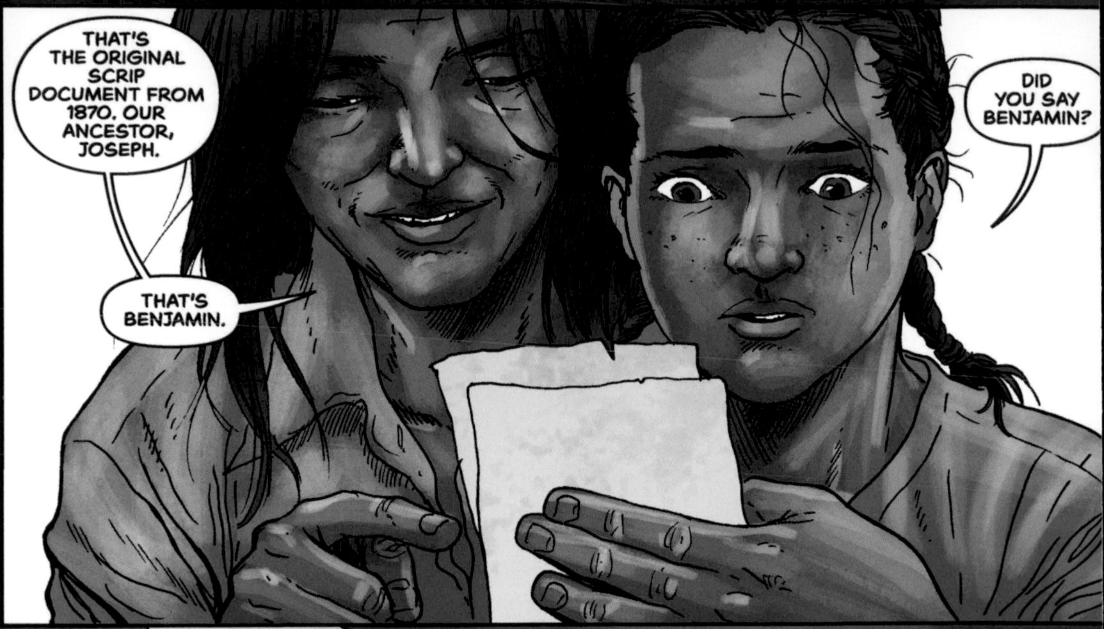
THAT'S THE ORIGINAL SCRIP DOCUMENT FROM 1870. OUR ANCESTOR, JOSEPH.
THAT'S BENJAMIN.
DID YOU SAY BENJAMIN?

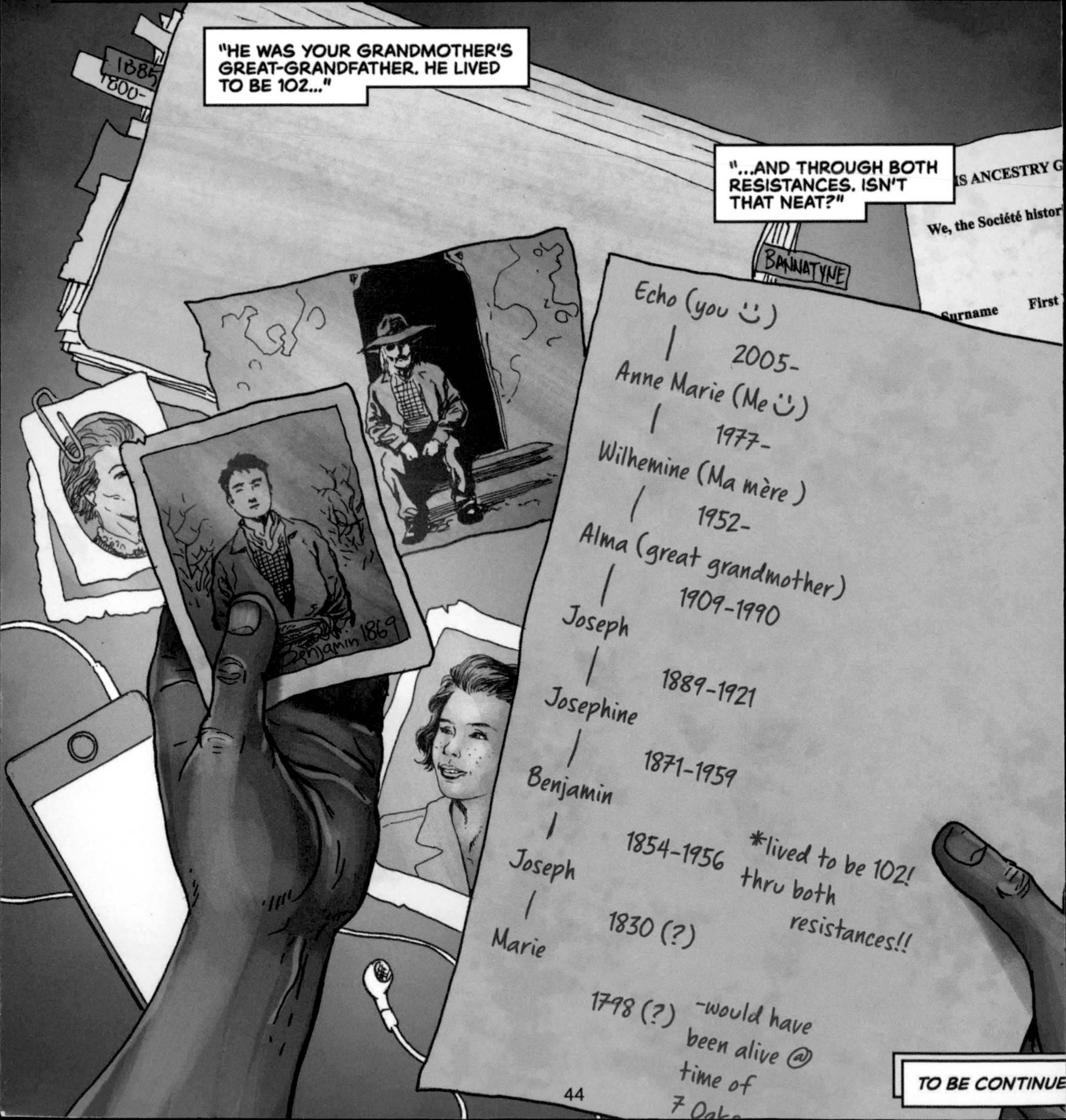
"HE WAS YOUR GRANDMOTHER'S GREAT-GRANDFATHER. HE LIVED TO BE 102..."
"...AND THROUGH BOTH RESISTANCES. ISN'T THAT NEAT?"
1885
1800-
IS ANCESTRY G
We, the Société histor
Surname
First
BANNATYNE
Benjamin 1869
Echo (you :))
2005-
Anne Marie (Me :))
1977-
Wilhemine (Ma mère)
1952-
Alma (great grandmother)
1909-1990
Joseph
1889-1921
Josephine
1871-1959
Benjamin
1854-1956
*lived to be 102! thru both resistances!!
Joseph
1830 (?)
Marie
1798 (?)
-would have been alive @ time of
TO BE CONTINUE

TIMELINE OF THE
NORTHWEST RESISTANCE

Following the Red River Resistance of 1870, things continued to change in the North-West Territory to the west. Many Métis had fled there from Red River, and settlers from Europe and the East were arriving daily. With the disappearance of the bison, the First Nations faced the end of their traditional way of life, yet the treaties that they signed with the Canadian government failed to deliver on their promises. They faced hunger and uncertainty. The Métis feared that title to their lands would not be honoured, and increased Anglo-Canadian settlement caused further unease. Many settlers had their own grievances with the government as well.

Out of this unrest came meetings, petitions, and delegations – all political actions designed to address these wrongs and seek redress from the Canadian government. At a meeting in March 1884, the Métis decided to invite Louis Riel back from exile. He and his family arrived in Batoche that summer.

1884
August 17 – Riel meets with Cree Chief Big Bear in Prince Albert to discuss coming together to present their peoples' concerns to the Canadian government.

Dec 16 – The first petition, outlining grievances and demands, is sent to the Secretary of State.

1885
March 17 – Chief One Arrow is invited to Batoche.

March 18 – While attempting to meet with Cree Chief One Arrow, Indian Agent John Lash is taken prisoner by the Métis. This is often cited as "one of the first overt acts of rebellion."

March 19 – Louis Riel petitions Métis, First Nations, and settlers to gather at Batoche on St. Joseph's Day to make a plan of action. Many wanted armed conflict. Those who don't leave. Riel declares a Provisional Government of Saskatchewan, with Batoche as its headquarters.

March 26 – At the Battle of Duck Lake, a force under the command of Gabriel Dumont outmaneuvers a newly mobilized Canadian force, causing them to retreat.

April 2 – After hearing about the success of Duck Lake, Big Bear's son Ayawasis and War Chief Wandering Spirit lead a raid on the settlers at the Catholic Church in Frog Lake, killing nine men, including Indian Agent Thomas Quinn.

April 13 – Ayawasis and Wandering Spirit's forces capture Fort Pitt. No one is killed, as Big Bear had warned the soldiers to flee before the attack.

April 24 – 200 Métis led by Dumont ambush the forces of General Middleton, commander of the North-West Field Force, and slow the Canadian advance towards Batoche, in the Battle of Fish Creek.

May 2 – Poundmaker's band overwhelms Colonel Otter's troops in the Battle of Cut Knife. Otter and the townspeople flee for Battleford.

– Dumont's men begin to dig rifle pits around Batoche, preparing to make a stand against Middleton's forces.

May 7 – The steamer *Northcote* arrives at Gabriel's crossing, near Batoche, carrying munitions including the infamous Gatling Gun, and Middleton's soldiers. They loot Dumont's house, using materials as fortifications on the boat.

May 9–12 – The Battle of Batoche:

May 9 – The first day of fighting.

– The steamer *Northcote* is crippled when a ferry cable lowered across the river is raised by the Métis forces, knocking down its smokestacks and sending the boat downriver, along with the precious Gatling Gun, and away from the fighting.

- The Canadians advance on land. Dumont sets fire to the prairie to stop them. But the land is too wet for the fires to go far enough. The soldiers outnumber the Métis four to one.

May 10 – Dumont builds a large half-moon trench in the middle of town.

May 11 – Middleton moves north to an open field at Jolie Prairie. Métis follow in rifle pits.

May 12 – Many Métis and Cree fighters are killed and wounded, leaving only 50 to 60 of the original force still fighting. They are running low on ammunition and under persistent fire from advanced Canadian artillery.

- Canadian forces charge Batoche, capturing the town.
- Under the guard of the Métis fighters, women, children, and others begin to flee along the river.

May 15 – Louis Riel surrenders to Middleton.

May 26 – Poundmaker and his councillors are arrested at Battleford. Poundmaker is tried for treason August 17 and sentenced to three years in Stony Mountain Penitentiary.

June 3 – The Battle of Loon Lake. Low on ammunition and supplies, Wandering Spirit surrenders to the North-West Mounted Police.

July 2 – Big Bear surrenders at Fort Carleton. Tried on September 11 for treason, he is sentenced to three years in Stony Mountain Penitentiary.

July 28 – Louis Riel's trial begins in Regina. He is found guilty of treason. Despite forceful public outcry in Francophone Canada and the jury's recommendations, Judge Hugh Richardson sentences Riel to death.

November 16 – Louis Riel is hanged at the Regina barracks of the North-West Mounted Police. His body is transported to Manitoba and he is buried at the Saint-Boniface Cathedral on December 12.

2019

May 23 – Poundmaker is exonerated by the Canadian government. Calls continue for the exoneration of chiefs Big Bear and One Arrow.

MANITOBA AND NORTHWEST TERRITORIES

DISTRICT OF
SASKATCHEWAN
Frog Lake
Fort Pitt
Prince Albert
North Saskatchewan River
Fort Carlton
Cut Knife
Duck Lake
Batoche
Fish Creek
Battleford
South Saskatchewan River
DISTRICT OF
ASSINIBOIA
MANITOBA
Moose Jaw
Regina
Stonewall
Canadian Pacific Railway
Winnipeg
Brandon
Fort Walsh
CANADA
U.S.A.
Grand Forks
MONTANA
NORTH DAKOTA
N
S
E
W

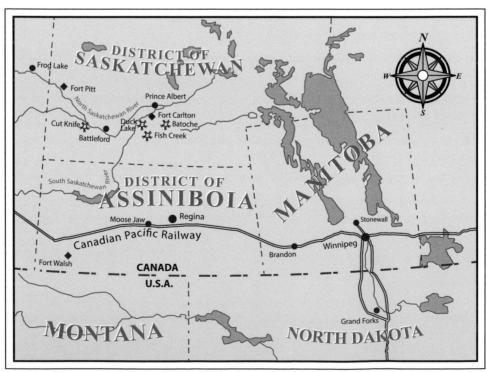

GABRIEL DUMONT
(1837–1906)

Gabriel Dumont was the Métis military leader during the Northwest Resistance. Born in the Red River Settlement to a family of prominent free traders and bison hunters, he fought his first battle at Grand Coteau when he was just 13 years old. He left Manitoba soon after the Red River Resistance, and became a Chief of the Hunt in the District of Saskatchewan. He was well known as a skilled diplomat and marksman, and he spoke seven languages.

The decline of the bison herds and rise of settlements prompted Dumont—as president of the Council of St. Laurent—to address the many challenges facing the Métis. In 1884, Dumont was a member of the delegation who traveled to Montana to convince Riel to lead the Métis in Saskatchewan.

In 1885, after the Canadian government refused to respond to dozens of petitions sent from the newly formed Provisional Government, led by Riel, residents called for armed response to ensure their rights to lands would be respected. The Northwest Resistance had begun, with Dumont as military leader and Riel as political leader. The Métis were finally outnumbered (250 to 1000) by Canadian forces at the Battle of Batoche (May 5 to 12, 1885).

Soon after the fall of Batoche, Dumont made his way to Montana and was soon joined by his wife Madeleine, who died the following year. After that, he had a brief stint performing with Buffalo Bill's Wild West Show, and traveled extensively around Quebec and the east coast of the United States. He did not return to Batoche until 1890.

REFERENCES

Dumont, Gabriel. Transl. by Michael Barnholden. *Gabriel Dumont Speaks*. Vancouver: Talonbooks, 2009.

Hildebrandt, Walter. *The Battle of Batoche: Small British Warfare and the Entrenched Métis*. Vancouver: Talonbooks, 2012.

LaPrairie, Jean. Ill. by Sheldon Dawson. *Times of Trouble: Based on the Memoirs of Isabelle Branconnier*. Illustrated Métis History Series. Winnipeg: Louis Riel Institute, 2010.

Teillet, Jean. *The North West Is Our Mother: The Story of Louis Riel's People, The Métis Nation*. Patrick Crean Editions. Toronto: HarperCollins Canada, 2019.

In memory of Lawrence Barkwell.

HighWater Press gratefully acknowledges the financial support of the Province of Manitoba through the Department of Culture, Heritage & Tourism and the Manitoba Book Publishing Tax Credit, and the Government of Canada through the Canada Book Fund (CBF) for our publishing activities.

The publisher also acknowledges the support of the Canada Council for the Arts, which last year invested $153 million to bring the arts to Canadians throughout the country.

Nous remercions le Conseil des arts du Canada de son soutien. L'an dernier, le Conseil a investi 153 millions de dollars pour mettre de l'art dans la vie des Canadiennes et des Canadiens de tout le pays.

Canada Council
for the Arts

Printed and bound in Canada by Friesens
Design by Relish New Brand Experience
Content reviewer: Lawrence Barkwell, Coordinator of Metis Heritage and History Research, Louis Riel Institute

Library and Archives Canada Cataloguing in Publication

Title: A girl called Echo. vol. 3, Northwest resistance / by Katherena Vermette ; illustrated by Scott B. Henderson ; coloured by Donovan Yaciuk.

Other titles: Northwest resistance

Names: Vermette, Katherena, 1977- author. | Henderson, Scott B., illustrator. | Yaciuk, Donovan, 1975- colourist.

Identifiers: Canadiana (print) 20190205148 | Canadiana (ebook) 20190205164 | ISBN 9781553798316 (softcover) | ISBN 9781553798934 (EPUB) | ISBN 9781553798941 (PDF)

Classification: LCC PN6733.V47 G57 2020 | DDC j741.5/971—dc23

23 22 21 20   1 2 3 4 5

HIGHWATER
PRESS

www.highwaterpress.com
Winnipeg, Manitoba
Treaty 1 Territory and homeland of the Métis Nation